Other Books by
RICHARD BRAUTIGAN

Novels

Trout Fishing in America
A Confederate General from Big Sur
In Watermelon Sugar
The Abortion: An Historical Romance 1966
The Hawkline Monster: A Gothic Western
Willard and His Bowling Trophies: A Perverse Mystery
Sombrero Fallout: A Japanese Novel

Poetry

The Galilee Hitch-Hiker*
Lay the Marble Tea*
The Octopus Frontier*
All Watched Over by Machines of Loving Grace*
Please Plant This Book
The Pill Versus the Springhill Mine Disaster
Rommel Drives on Deep into Egypt
Loading Mercury with a Pitchfork
June 3oth, June 3oth

Short Stories

Revenge of the Lawn

*out of print

RICHARD BRAUTIGAN

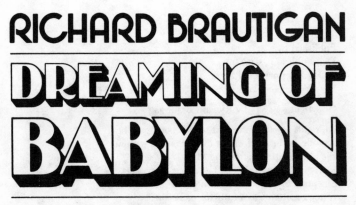

DREAMING OF BABYLON

A Private Eye Novel 1942

A DELTA BOOK

A DELTA BOOK

Published by
Dell Publishing Co., Inc.
1 Dag Hammarskjold Plaza
New York, New York 10017

ISBN: 0-440-52059-2

Manufactured in the United States of America

Fourth printing—September 1980

V B

This one is for Helen Brann
with love from Richard.

I guess one of the reasons
that I've never been
a very good private detective
is that I spend too much time
dreaming of Babylon.

What Happened to C. Card in Early 1942:

Good News,
Bad News

        January 2, 1942 had some good news and some
bad news.

First, the good news: I found out that I was 4F and wasn't
going off to World War II to be a soldier boy. I didn't feel
unpatriotic at all because I had fought my World War II five
years before in Spain and had a couple of bullet holes in my
ass to prove it.

I'll never figure out why I got shot in the ass. Anyway, it
made a lousy war story. People don't look up to you as a hero
when you tell them you were shot in the ass. They don't take
you seriously but that wasn't my problem any more at all.
The war that was starting for the rest of America was over
for me.

Now for the bad news: I didn't have any bullets for my gun. I had just gotten a case that I needed my gun for but I was fresh out of bullets. The client that I was going to meet later on in the day for the first time wanted me to show up with a gun and I knew that an empty gun was not what they had in mind.

What was I going to do?

I didn't have a cent to my name and my credit in San Francisco wasn't worth two bits. I had to give up my office in September, though it only cost eight bucks a month, and now I was just working out of the pay telephone in the front hall of the cheap apartment building I was living in on Nob Hill where I was two months behind in my rent. I couldn't even come up with thirty bucks a month.

My landlady was a bigger threat to me than the Japanese. Everybody was waiting for the Japanese to show up in San Francisco and start taking cable cars up and down the hills, but believe me I would have taken on a division of them to get my landlady off my back.

"Where in the hell is my rent, you deadbeat!" she'd yell at me from the top of the stairs where her apartment was. She was always wearing a loose bathrobe that covered up a body that would have won first prize in a beauty contest for cement blocks.

"The country's at war and you don't even pay your God-damn rent!"

She had a voice that made Pearl Harbor seem like a lullaby.

"Tomorrow," I'd lie to her.

"Tomorrow your ass!" she'd yell back.

She was about sixty and had been married five times and

widowed five times: the lucky sons-of-bitches. That's how she'd come to own the apartment building. One of them left it to her. God had done him a favor when He stalled his car one rainy night on some railroad tracks just outside of Merced. He had been a travelling salesman: brushes. After the train hit his car they couldn't tell the difference between him and his brushes. I think they buried him with some of his brushes in the coffin, believing they were part of him.

In those ancient long-ago days when I paid my rent, she was very friendly to me and used to invite me into her apartment for coffee and doughnuts. She loved to talk about her dead husbands, especially one of them who'd been a plumber. She liked to talk about how good he was at fixing hot water heaters. Her other four husbands were always out of focus when she talked about them. It was as if the marriages had taken place in murky aquariums. Even her husband who'd been hit by the train didn't merit much comment from her, but she couldn't say enough about the guy who could fix the hot water heaters. I think he was pretty good at fixing her hot water heater, too.

The coffee she served was always very weak and the doughnuts slightly stale because she bought day-old stuff at a bakery a few blocks away on California Street.

I'd have coffee with her sometimes because I didn't have much to do, anyway. Things were just as slow then as they are now except for the case I just got but I had saved up a little money that I'd gotten from being in an automobile accident and settling out of court, so I could still pay my rent, though I'd given up my office a few months before.

In April 1941 I had to let my secretary go. I hated to do that. I spent the five months she worked for me trying to

3

get her in the sack. She was friendly but I barely got to first base with her. We did some kissing at the office but that was about it.

After I had to let her go, she told me to buzz off.

I called her up one night and her parting shot at me over the telephone went something like this: ". . . and besides not being a good kisser, you're a lousy detective. You should try another line of work. Bellboy would suit you perfectly."

CLICK

Oh, well . . .

She had a lard ass, anyway. The only reason I hired her was because she would work for the lowest wages this side of Chinatown.

I sold my car in July.

Anyway, here I was with no bullets for my gun and no money to get any and no credit and nothing left to pawn. I was sitting in my cheap little apartment on Leavenworth Street in San Francisco thinking this over when suddenly hunger started working my stomach over like Joe Louis. Three good right hooks to my gut and I was on my way over to the refrigerator.

That was a big mistake.

I looked inside and then hurriedly closed the door when the jungle foliage inside tried to escape. I don't know how people can live the way I do. My apartment is so dirty that recently I replaced all the seventy-five-watt bulbs with twenty-five-watters, so I wouldn't have to see it. It was a luxury but I had to do it. Fortunately, the apartment didn't have any windows or I might have really been in trouble.

My apartment was so dim that it looked like the shadow of an apartment. I wonder if I always lived like this. I mean,

I had to have had a mother, somebody to tell me to clean up, take care of myself, change my socks. I did, too, but I guess I was kind of slow when I was a kid and didn't catch on. There had to be a reason.

I stood there beside the refrigerator wondering what to do next when I got a great idea. What did I have to lose? I didn't have any money for bullets and I was hungry. I needed something to eat.

I went upstairs to my landlady's apartment.

I rang the doorbell.

This would be the last thing in the world that she would expect because I'd spent over a month now trying to elude her like an eel but always being caught in a net of curses.

When she answered the door she couldn't believe that I was standing there. She looked as if her doorknob had been electrified. She was actually speechless. I took full advantage of it.

"Eureka!" I yelled into her face. "I can pay the rent! I can buy the building! How much do you want for it? Twenty thousand cash! My ship has come in! Oil! Oil!"

She was so confused that she beckoned me to come into her apartment and pointed out a chair for me to sit down in. She still hadn't said a word. I was really cooking. I could hardly believe myself.

I went into the apartment.

"Oil! Oil!" I continued yelling, and then I started making motions like oil gushing from the ground. I turned into an oil well right in front of her eyes.

I sat down.

She sat down opposite me.

Her mouth was still glued shut.

"My uncle discovered oil in Rhode Island!" I yelled across at her. "I own half of it. I'm rich. Twenty thousand cash for this pile of shit you call an apartment building! Twenty-five thousand!" I yelled. "I want to marry you and raise a whole family of little apartment buildings! I want our wedding certificate printed on a No Vacancy sign!"

It worked.

She believed me.

Five minutes later I had a cup of very weak coffee in my hand and I was munching on a stale doughnut and she was telling me how happy she was for me. I told her that I would buy the building from her next week when the first million dollars' worth of oil royalties arrived.

When I left her apartment with hunger abated and another week's housing assured, she shook my hand and said, "You're a good boy. Oil in Rhode Island."

"That's right," I said. "Near Hartford."

I was going to ask her for five dollars so that I could buy some bullets for my gun but I figured I'd better let well enough alone.

Ha-ha.

Get the joke?

Babylon

Uh-oh, I started dreaming of Babylon as I walked back down the stairs to my apartment. It was very important that I not dream of Babylon just as I was starting to get some things worked out. If I got started on Babylon whole hours would pass without my knowing it.

I could sit down in my apartment and suddenly it would be midnight and I would have lost the edge on getting my life back together again whose immediate need was some bullets for my gun.

The last thing in the world that I needed right now was to start dreaming of Babylon.

I had to hold Babylon back for a while, long enough for me to get some bullets. I made an heroic effort as I walked down the stairs of the musty, seedy, tomb-like smelling apartment building to keep Babylon at arm's reach.

It was touch and go there for a few seconds and then Babylon floated back into the shadows, away from me.

I felt a little sad.

I didn't want Babylon to go.

Oklahoma

I went into my apartment and got my gun. *I should clean this thing someday*, I thought, as I put it into my coat pocket. Also, I should probably get a shoulder holster. That would be an authentic touch that might help me get more cases.

When I left my apartment to go out into San Francisco to hustle some bullets, my landlady was standing at the top of the stairs, waiting for me.

Oh, God, I thought. She's come to her senses. I waited for a huge tirade of curses to bombard my ears and bring my life back to hell on earth again, but it didn't happen. She just stood there watching me as I walked out of the building with a frozen smile on my face.

Just as I was opening the front door, she spoke. Her voice was almost child-like. "Why not oil wells in Oklahoma?" she said. "There's a lot of oil in Oklahoma."

"Too close to Texas," I said. "Salt water flows under the highway."

That finished her off.

There was no reply.

She looked like Alice in Wonderland.

Cactus Fog

There was no place that I was going to get any
money to buy bullets, so I decided to go where there are
always bullets: a police station.

I walked down to the Hall of Justice on Kearny Street to
see a detective that I knew down there and once had been
very good friends with to see if I could borrow some bullets
from him.

Maybe he would loan me six until I met my client and
got an advance. I was supposed to meet them in front of a
radio station down on Powell Street. It was now 2 P.M. I had
four hours to get some bullets. I hadn't the slightest idea
who my client was or what they wanted done except that I
was to meet them in front of the radio station at six and then

they would tell me what they wanted done and I'd try to get an advance from them.

Then I'd give my landlady a few bucks and tell her that an armored car bringing me the million dollars had gotten lost in a cactus fog near Phoenix, Arizona, but she shouldn't worry because the fog was guaranteed to lift any day now and then the money would be on its way.

If she asked me what a cactus fog was, I'd tell her it was the worst kind of fog because it had sharp spines on it. It made moving around in it a very dangerous proposition. It was best to stay where you were at and just wait until it went away.

The million dollars is waiting for the fog to pass.

My Girlfriend

It was a fast hike down to the Hall of Justice. I'd gotten used to walking in San Francisco and could move around at a good clip.

I started 1941 off with a car and now a year later, here I was totally relying on my feet. Life has its ups and downs. The only place my life could go now was up. The only thing lower than me was a dead man.

It was a cold windy day in San Francisco but I enjoyed the walk down Nob Hill to the Hall of Justice.

I started to think about Babylon as I neared Chinatown but was able to change the marquee in my mind just in time. I saw some Chinese kids playing in the street. I tried to figure out what kind of game they were playing. By concentrating on the kids, I was able to avoid Babylon rolling toward me like a freight train.

Whenever I was trying to get something done and Babylon started coming upon me I'd try to focus on anything that could keep it away. It was always very hard because I really like to dream of Babylon and I have a beautiful girlfriend there. This is a hard thing to admit but I like her better than real girls. I've always wanted to meet a girl that interested me as much as my friend in Babylon.

I don't know.

Maybe someday.

Maybe never.

Sergeant Rink

After the Chinese kids' game I thought about my detective friend to keep Babylon away. He was a sergeant and his name was Rink. He was a very tough cop. I think he held the world's record for being tough. He had perfected a slap across the face that left an exact hand print on it like a temporary brand. That slap was just a friendly greeting from Sergeant Rink compared to how things got later on if you weren't very, very cooperative.

I met Rink when we were both trying out for the force back in '36. I wanted to be a cop. We were very good friends back then. We might be on the force together right now, partners solving murders, if only I had managed to pass the final examination. My score was close, though. I was just five points away from being a cop.

Dreaming of Babylon got the best of me. I would have been a good cop, too. If only I had been able to stop dreaming of Babylon. Babylon has been such a delight to me and at the same time such a curse.

I didn't answer the last twenty questions of the test. That's why I failed. I just sat there dreaming of Babylon while everybody else answered the questions and became policemen.

The Hall of Justice

I never really cared about the way the Hall of Justice looks. It's a huge, tomb-like gloomy-looking building and inside it always smells like rotten marble.

I don't know.

Maybe it's just me.

Probably.

One interesting thing, though, is: I've been in the Hall of Justice a couple of hundred times at least and I never think about Babylon when I'm there, so it does serve some purpose for me.

I took the elevator up to the fourth floor and found my detective friend sitting at his desk in the homicide department. My friend resembles exactly what he is: a very tough cop who's interested in solving murder cases. The only thing he likes better than a nice juicy homicide is a sirloin steak smothered with onions. He was in his early thirties and built like a Dodge pickup.

The first thing I noticed was his shoulder holster with a nice-looking .38 police special resting comfortably in it. I was particularly attracted to the bullets in the gun. I would have liked all six of them but settled for three.

Sergeant Rink was very carefully examining a letter opener.

He looked up.

"A sight for sore eyes," he said.

"What do you need a letter opener for?" I said, slipping into the genre. "You know that reading isn't one of your gifts."

"Still selling dirty pictures?" he said, smiling. "Tijuana valentines? The ones for dog lovers?"

"No," I said. "Too many cops kept asking for samples. They cleaned me out."

The private detective business was very slow one time when the Worlds Fair was going on over at Treasure Island in '40, so I supplemented my income by selling a few "art" photographs to the tourists.

Sergeant Rink always liked to kid me about them.

I've done a lot of things in my life that I haven't been proud of, but the worst thing I ever did was getting as poor as I was now.

"This is a murder weapon," Rink said, dropping the letter opener on his desk. "It was found in a prostitute's back early this morning. No clues. Only her body in a doorway and this."

"The murderer was confused," I said. "Somebody should have taken them to a stationery store and pointed out the difference between an envelope and a whore."

"Oh, boy," Rink said, shaking his head.

He picked up the letter opener again.

He turned it very slowly over in his hand. Watching him play with a murder weapon wasn't getting me any closer to some bullets for my gun.

"What do you want?" he said, staring at the letter opener, not bothering to look up at me. "You know the last time I loaned you a buck I said that was it, so what do you want? What can I do for you except give you directions to the Golden Gate Bridge and a few basics on how to jump? When are you going to give up this silly notion of you being a private detective and get a paying job and out of my hair? There's a war going on. They need everybody. There must be something you can do."

"I need your help," I said.

"Ah, shit," he said, finally looking up. He put the letter opener down and reached into his pocket and took out a handful of change. He very carefully selected two quarters, two dimes and a nickel. He put them down on the desk and then pushed them toward me.

"That's it," he said. "Last year you were worth five bucks, then you dropped to one. Now you're a seventy-five-center. Get a job. For Christ's sake. There must be something you can do. I know one thing for sure: detective work isn't it. Not many people want to hire a detective who's only wearing one sock. You could probably count them on your hand."

I was hoping that Rink wouldn't notice that, but of course

he had. I was thinking about Babylon in the morning when I got dressed and didn't notice that I was only wearing one sock until I walked into the Hall of Justice.

I was going to tell Rink that I didn't need the seventy-five cents, which of course I did, but what I really wanted was some bullets for my gun.

I tried to size up the situation.

I had limited options.

I could take the seventy-five cents and be ahead of the game or I could say: No, I don't want the money. What I want is some bullets for my gun.

If I took the seventy-five cents and then asked him for the bullets, he might really blow his stack. I had to be very careful because as I said earlier: He was one of my friends. You can imagine what the people who didn't like me were like.

I looked at the seventy-five cents on his desk.

Then I remembered a minor criminal I knew who lived in North Beach. As I remembered he had a gun once. Maybe he still had it and I could get some bullets for my gun from him.

I picked up the seventy-five cents.

"Thank you," I said.

Rink sighed.

"Get your ass out of here," he said. "The next time I see you I want to be looking at an employed man who's eager to repay eighty-three dollars and seventy-five cents to his old friend Rink. If I see anything that resembles you the way you are now, I'll vag you and make sure you get thirty days. Pull yourself together and get the fuck out of here."

I left him playing with the letter opener.

Maybe it would give him an idea for a lead that would solve the case of the murdered prostitute.

Also, maybe, he could take it and shove it up his ass.

Adolf Hitler

I left the Hall of Justice and walked up to North Beach to see if I could get some bullets out of the minor criminal I knew who lived on Telegraph Hill.

He lived in an apartment on Green Street.

Just my luck the minor crook wasn't home. His mother answered the door. I had never met her before but I knew it was his mother because he had talked a lot about her. She took one look at me and said, "He's gone straight. Go away. He's a good boy now. Find somebody else to break into places with."

"What?" I said.

"You know what," she said. "He doesn't want to have

anything to do with guys like you. He goes to church now. Six o'clock Mass."

She was a little old Italian lady about sixty. She was wearing a white apron. I think she misunderstood what type of person I was.

"He's gone down to join the Army," she said. "He can, you know. He never got into any real trouble. Just little things. Guys like you made him do it. He's going to fight Adolf Hitler. Show that son-of-a-bitch what's what."

Then she started to close the door.

"Get out of here!" she yelled. "Go join the Army! Make something of yourself! It's not too late! The recruiting office is open right now! They'll take you if you haven't been in the pen!"

"I don't think you know who I am. I'm a private—"
SLAM!

It was an obvious misunderstanding.

Amazing.

She thought I was a crook.

I'd just come there to borrow a few bullets.

Mustard

Still no bullets, and I was getting hungry. The nutrition from the stale doughnut I had cadged from my landlady was rapidly becoming a thing of the past.

I went into a little Italian delicatessen on Columbus Avenue and got a salami and Swiss cheese sandwich on a French roll with lots of mustard.

I like it that way: lots and lots of mustard.

It put a forty-five-cent dent in my seventy-five cents.

I was now a thirty-cent private detective.

The old Italian who made the sandwich for me was very interesting looking. Anyway, I made him look interesting because I started to think about Babylon, and I couldn't

afford to if I was going to earn some money from my first
client since October 13, 1941.

Jesus, what a dry spell!

That had been a divorce case.

A three-hundred-pound husband wanted the goods on his
three-hundred-pound wife. He thought that she was fooling
around and she was: with a three-hundred-pound automobile mechanic. Some case. She used to go down to his garage
every Wednesday afternoon and he'd fuck her over the hood
of a car. I got some terrific photographs. That was before I
had to pawn my camera. You should have seen the expression on their faces when I jumped out from behind a Buick
and started snapping away. When he pulled out of her she
rolled right over onto the floor and made a sound like an
elevator falling on an elephant.

"Put a little more mustard on it," I said.

"You sure likea the mustard," the old Italian said. "You
shoulda ordera plain mustard sandwich." He laughed when
he said that.

"Maybe your next customer won't want any," I said. "He
might be a mustard hater. Can't stand the stuff Would
sooner go to China."

"I surea hope so," he said. "I go outa business. No more
sandwiches."

The old Italian looked just like Rudolph Valentino if
Rudolph Valentino had been an old Italian making sandwiches and complaining about people having too much mustard on their sandwiches.

What's wrong with liking mustard?

I could like six-year-old girls.

Bela Lugosi

I walked back down Columbus Avenue, eating my sandwich and headed toward the morgue. I had remembered another place where I might get some bullets. It was a long shot but everything I did these days was a long shot, starting off when I woke up in the morning. The odds were 50–1 against me taking my morning piss without getting half a bladder on my foot, if you know what I mean.

I had a friend who worked at the morgue. He kept a gun in his desk. I thought it was sort of strange when I first got to know the guy. I mean, what in the hell do you need a gun for in a place filled with dead bodies? The chances are very slim that Bela Lugosi and some of his friends, like Igor, are going to break into the place and make off with some stiffs to bring back to life.

One day I asked my friend about the gun.

He didn't say anything for a few minutes.

He was really thinking about it.

"They brought in this dead ax murderer," he said, finally. "Who'd been shot by the police after beheading all the participants of a card game that he held every Friday night for twenty years in his basement. He was running around in the street waving his ax when the police pumped eight bullets into him. When the police brought him in here, he sure looked dead to me, but it didn't quite work out that way. I was putting him in the cooler when suddenly he sat up and tried to chop my head off with his hand. He still thought he had an ax in it. I hit him over the head with an autopsy pan and that quieted him down. He was really dead by the time the police got here after I called them.

"That caused an embarrassing situation because they didn't believe me. They thought I'd had a drink or two and imagined the whole thing.

" 'No,' I said. 'You guys brought somebody in here who wasn't dead. I mean, this son-of-a-bitch was still kicking.'

"Then your friend Rink who was with them said, 'Peg-leg, let me ask you a question.'

" 'Sure,' I said.

" 'And I want you to answer this question as truthfully as you can. OK?'

" 'OK,' I said. 'Shoot.'

" 'Do you see a lot of bullet holes in this bastard?'

" 'Yeah,' I said.

" 'Is he dead now?'

"We were all standing around the body. He had so many bullet holes in him that it was ridiculous.

" 'Yeah,' I said.

" 'Are you sure he's dead?'

" 'Positive,' I said.

" 'Positive?' Rink said.

" 'Positive,' I said.

" 'Then forget about it,' he said.

" 'You don't believe me?' I said.

" 'We believe you,' he said. 'But don't tell anybody else. I wouldn't even tell your wife.'

" 'I'm not married,' I said.

" 'Even a better reason not to.'

"Then they left.

"They all took a good long look at me before they left. I got the message but still that son-of-a-bitch had been alive, so I didn't want to take any more chances with all the dead murderers, bank robbers and maniacs that come in here. You never know when they're not dead, when they're just playacting or unconscious or something and they might suddenly attack you, so I got the gun I keep here in the desk. I'm prepared now. The next time: BANG!"

That's where I'd borrow the bullets I needed.

I'd get them from my friend Peg-leg who works at the morgue and keeps a gun around to shoot dead people.

1934

Suddenly I remembered that earlier in the day I was supposed to make a phone call but I didn't have a nickel then, but now I did, thanks to Sergeant Rink, so I stopped at a telephone booth and made the call.

The person I was supposed to call wasn't home and the telephone didn't return my nickel. I hit it a half-a-dozen times with my fist and called it a son-of-a-bitch. That didn't work either. Then I noticed some mustard on the receiver and I felt a little better.

I'd have to call again later on and my original seventy-five cents was busy wasting away. This could be very funny if it was a laughing matter.

Anyway, I wasn't hungry, any more.

Got to keep looking at the bright side.

Can't let it get to me.

If it really gets to me I start thinking about Babylon and then it only gets worse because I'd sooner think about Babylon than anything else and when I start thinking about Babylon I can't do anything but think about Babylon and my whole life falls to pieces.

Anyway, that's what it's been doing for the last eight years, ever since 1934, which was when I started thinking about Babylon.

The Blonde

When I walked into the morgue just behind the Hall of Justice on Merchant Street, a young woman was walking out crying. She was wearing a fur coat. She looked like a very fancy dame. She had short blonde hair, a long nose and a mouth that looked so good that my lips started aching.

I hadn't kissed anyone in a long time. It's hard to find people to kiss when you haven't got any money in your pocket and you're as big a fuckup as I am.

I hadn't kissed anybody since the day before Pearl Harbor. That was Mabel. I'll go into my love life later on when nothing else is happening. I mean, absolutely nothing: zero.

The blonde looked at me as she came down the stairs. She

looked at me as if she knew me but she didn't say anything. She just continued crying.

I looked over my shoulder to see if there was somebody else behind me that she might be looking at, but I was the only person going into the morgue, so it had to be me. That was strange.

I turned around and watched her walk away.

She stopped at the curb and a chauffeur-driven 16-cylinder black Cadillac LaSalle limousine pulled up beside her and she got in. The car seemed to come out of nowhere. It wasn't there and then it was there. She was staring out the window at me as the car drove away.

Her chauffeur was a very large and mean-looking gent. He had a Jack Dempsey–type face and a huge neck. He looked as if he'd get a lot of pleasure out of going ten rounds with your grandmother and making sure she went the whole distance. Afterwards you could take her home in a gallon jar.

As the limousine drove away he turned and gave me a big smile as if we shared a secret: old buddies or something.

I'd never seen him before.

"Eye"

I found my morgue pal Peg-leg back in the autopsy room staring at the dead breasts of a lady corpse lying on a stone table, obviously waiting to get her very own autopsy. You only get one in this world.

He was thoroughly engrossed in staring at her tits.

She was a good-looking woman but she was dead.

"Aren't you a little old for that?" I said.

"Oh, 'Eye,' " Peg-leg said. "Haven't you starved to death yet? I've been waiting to get your body."

Peg-leg always called me "Eye." That was short for private eye.

"My luck's changing," I said. "I got a client."

"That's funny," Peg-leg said. "I read the paper this morning and I didn't see anything about any inmates escaping from the local asylums. Why did the person choose you? They've got real detectives in San Francisco. They're in the phone book."

I looked at Peg-leg and then at the corpse of the young woman. She had been very beautiful in life. Dead, she looked dead.

"I think if I'd come in here a few minutes from now, you'd be humping your girlfriend there," I said. "You ought to try a live one sometime. You don't catch a cold everytime you fuck them."

Peg-leg smiled and continued admiring the dead broad.

"A perfect body," he said, sighing. "The only flaw is a five-inch-deep hole in her back. Somebody stuck a letter opener in her. A real shame."

"She was stabbed with a letter opener?" I asked. That rang a bell but I couldn't place it. Somehow it was familiar.

"Yeah, she was a lady of the night. They found her in a doorway. What a waste of talent."

"Have you ever gone to bed with a living woman?" I said. "What would your mother think if she knew you were doing things like this?"

"My mother doesn't think. She's still living with my father. What do you want, 'Eye?' You know your credit isn't any good but if you want a place to sleep, there's an empty bunk downstairs in cold storage, waiting for you, or I can tuck you in up here." He motioned his head toward an eerie-looking refrigerator built into the wall that had enough space for four dead bodies.

Most of the bodies were kept downstairs in "cold storage," but they kept a few special ones in the autopsy room.

"Thanks, but I don't want any perverts staring at me while I'm sleeping."

"How about some coffee, then?" Peg-leg asked.

"Sure," I said.

We went over to his desk that was in the corner of the autopsy room. He had a hot plate on the desk. We poured ourselves some coffee from a pot and sat down.

"OK, 'Eye,' spill it. You didn't come down here because you wanted to pay back the fifty bucks you borrowed from me. Right? Right," he answered himself.

I took a sip of coffee. It tasted like he got it out of the asshole of one of his corpse friends. I was going to say that but I changed my mind.

"I need some bullets," I said.

"Oh, boy," Peg-leg said. "Repeat that."

"I've got a case, a client, cash money, but the job requires that I pack a piece."

"You carry a gun?" he said. "Isn't that kind of dangerous?"

"I was in the war," I said. "I was a soldier. I got wounded. I'm a hero."

"Bullshit! You fought for those fucking Communists in Spain and got shot in the ass. It serves you right, too. How did you get shot in the ass?"

I returned the conversation to its original subject. I didn't have all day to spend with this joker.

"I need six bullets," I said. "My gun's empty. I don't think my client would want to hire a private detective who carries an empty gun. Don't you have a gun you keep here in case stiffs get up and and start chasing you with axes?"

"Not so loud," Peg-leg said, looking around, though there

wasn't anybody else in the room. He had taken Sergeant Rink's advice about not telling people about the ax-murderer incident very seriously. I was one of the few people that he had told about it. We were pretty close friends until I started borrowing money from him and couldn't repay it. We were still friends but he wanted his money, so there was kind of like a short wall between us. It wasn't serious but it was there.

"Well?" I said.

"Yeah, I've still got it here. You never know."

"Will you loan me some bullets, then? Six would do fine."

"First, you start out borrowing tens, then you switch to fives, then it's ones and now you want the bullets from my fucking gun. You take the cake. You are a loser. A real loser."

"I know that," I said. "But I need some bullets. How can I ever pay you back if you don't loan me enough ammunition so that I can go to work?"

Peg-leg looked slightly disgusted.

"Oh, shit," he said. "But I'm not going to give them all to you. I'm going to keep three of them for myself just in case something weird happens around here again."

"You still think that was real, huh?" I said.

"Watch it, 'Eye,' " Peg-leg said.

He took another look around the room. We were still alone. He pulled the drawer of his desk out very cautiously and removed a revolver. He opened up the cylinder and took out three bullets and gave them to me. Then he put the revolver away.

"Deadbeat," he said.

I looked at the cartridges in my hand. Actually, I was staring at them.

"What's wrong?" he said.

"What caliber are these?" I said.

".32s," he said.

"Ah, shit!" I said.

.38

"You've got a .38, right?" Peg-leg said.

"How did you guess?"

"Knowing you it wasn't hard."

"What am I going to do?" I said.

"Why don't you get a job?" Peg-leg said. "A lot of people work. It's not like leprosy."

"But I've got a client," I said. "A real client."

"You've had clients before and you've been fired before. Face it, pal. You're not any good at this private detective business. If my wife was cheating I'd hire Donald Duck to find out who she was doing it with before I'd hire you, and I'm not even married. Why don't you buy some bullets for your God-damn gun?"

"I don't have any money," I said.

"Not even enough to buy some bullets? Hell, they only cost a dollar or so."

"I've fallen on hard times," I said.

"I think the only good times I ever saw you have was when you got hit by a car last year," Peg-leg said. "And some people don't consider being hit by a car and breaking both your legs good luck."

"What am I going to do?" I said.

Peg-leg shook his head and smiled painfully.

He opened the desk drawer and took out his gun and handed it to me.

"If some dead stranger comes back to life and throttles me while I'm trying to wash their face, it'll be your fucking fault and I'll come back and haunt you. You'll never get a decent night's sleep again. I'll be flapping my sheet right up your asshole. You'll be sorry."

I put the gun in my coat pocket that didn't already have a gun in it.

"Thanks a lot, Peg-leg," I said. "You're a true-blue pal."

"You're a total fuckup," Peg-leg said. "I want to see that gun back here tomorrow morning."

"Thank you," I said, feeling like a real private detective with a loaded gun in my pocket. My luck was definitely changing. I was on my way up.

The Morning Mail

Peg-leg walked me out to the front door. He moved quickly and gracefully for a man with a peg-leg. Did I mention that before? I don't think I did. I should have. It's kind of interesting: a man with a peg-leg taking care of dead people.

Then I remembered something that I was going to ask him.

"Hey, Peg-leg," I said. "Did you see that blonde who came out of here a little while ago? She had short hair, a fur coat, real good-looking."

"Yeah," he said. "She was here visiting one of my clients: the good-looker that somebody used as a substitute because they couldn't wait to open their morning mail."

"What?" I said.

"The letter-opener job."

"Did you say a letter opener?" I asked.

"Yeah, the girl who was killed with the letter opener. The blonde saw her. She said she thought the girl might be her sister. She read about it in the newspaper but it turned out she was the wrong girl."

"That's funny," I said. "She was crying when she went out the door."

"I don't know anything about that but she wasn't crying when she left me. She was very unemotional. A cold fish," Peg-leg said.

The letter opener!

Now I remembered.

Sergeant Rink was playing with the letter opener that killed the girl I had just seen Peg-leg drooling over. I knew when Peg-leg first mentioned a letter opener that it rang some kind of bell and this was it. The letter opener was the murder weapon.

A bunch of amateur coincidences for no particular reason, I thought, *but they don't have anything to do with me.*

"Good-bye," I said.

"Don't forget to bring the gun back tomorrow morning," Peg-leg said, peg-legging it back into the morgue.

The Boss

Hurray, I had a loaded gun! In a few hours I would be able to meet my client with confidence in my step. I wondered what they wanted me to do that required a gun. Oh, well, beggars can't be choosers. I really needed the money.

I was going to ask for fifty dollars expense money. That would go a long way in changing my circumstances. I could get the landlady off my back with a few bucks. I didn't think that story I fed her about oil wells in Rhode Island had much longevity. I figured by the time I got back to the apartment, she'd be howling away like a banshee.

I had some time to kill, so I walked up the street to

Portsmouth Square and sat down on a bench near the statue dedicated to Robert Louis Stevenson.

A lot of Chinese were coming and going in the park. I watched them for a while. Interesting people. Very energetic. I wondered if anyone had ever told them that they looked just like Japanese and it was not a good time to look like Japanese.

That didn't have anything to do with me any more because my war was over, so I thought, sitting there on a park bench in San Francisco, letting the world go by. I had a loaded gun in my pocket and a client that was willing to pay for my services.

The world wasn't such a bad place, so I started thinking about Babylon. Why not? I didn't have anything else to do for a couple of hours. It couldn't hurt. I'd just have to be very careful about dreaming of Babylon. I wouldn't let it get the best of me. I'd stay on top of it. That's what I would do.

I'd show Babylon who was boss.

The Front Door
to Babylon

I guess I should give you a little background about my involvement with Babylon. I was out of high school and looking around for something to do with my life.

I'd been a pretty fair baseball player in high school. I lettered two years in a row and hit .320 in my senior year, including four home runs, so I decided to try my hand at professional baseball.

I tried out one afternoon for a semi-pro team and figured that it was the beginning of a career that would take me to the New York Yankees. I was a first baseman, so the Yankees would have to get rid of Lou Gehrig who was playing first base for them, then, but I figured that the better man would win out and that was of course me.

When I arrived at the ball park to try out for the team, the first thing the manager said to me was, "You don't look like a first baseman."

"Looks are deceiving. Watch me play. I'm the best."

The manager shook his head.

"I don't think I've even seen a baseball player that looks like you. Are you sure you've played first base?"

"Put a bat in my hand and I'll show you who I am."

"OK," the manager said. "But you'd better not waste my time. We're in second place, just a game out of first."

I didn't know what that had to do with me but I pretended that I appreciated the significance of this achievement.

"You'll be five games in first place after I take over first base," I said, humoring the son-of-a-bitch.

There were about a dozen halfwit-looking baseball players standing around playing catch and shooting the breeze with each other.

The manager motioned toward one of them.

"Hey, Sam!" he yelled. "Come over here and throw a few balls at this guy. He thinks he's Lou Gehrig."

"How'd you know?" I said.

"If you're wasting my time, I'll personally toss your ass out of this ball park," the manager said.

I could see that him and me were never going to be friends, but I'd show the bastard. He'd be eating his own words soon enough.

I picked up a baseball bat and walked up to home plate. I felt very confident.

Sam, the pitcher, took his place on the mound. He was a very unimpressive-looking pitcher. He was about twenty-five and had a slight build hanging awkwardly on a six-foot frame. I don't think he weighed over a 130 soaking wet with a bowling ball in his lap.

"Is that the best you've got!" I yelled at the manager.

"Sam!" the manager yelled. "Put some smoke on it for this kid!"

Sam smiled.

He was never going to make it in the movies. He had a pair of buckteeth that made him look like the first cousin of a walrus.

I took some practice swings. Then Sam very slowly wound up. He took the longest time to wind up. He was like a snake uncoiling. The smile never left his face.

That's the last thing I remembered before being in Babylon.

President Roosevelt

It was really beautiful in Babylon. I went for a long walk beside the Euphrates River. There was a girl with me. She was very beautiful and wearing a gown that I could see her body through. She had on an emerald necklace.

We talked about President Roosevelt. She was a Democrat, too. The fact that she had large firm breasts and was a Democrat made her the perfect woman for me.

"I wish that President Roosevelt was my father," she said in a husky voice like honey. "If President Roosevelt was my dad, I'd cook breakfast for him every morning. I make a very good waffle."

What a gal!
What a gal!
By the banks of the Euphrates in Babylon
What a gal!

It was just like a song being played on the radio in my mind.

A Babylonian
Sand Watch

"How do you make your waffles?" I said.

"I use two eggs," she said, and then suddenly looked at her watch. It was a Babylonian sand watch. It had twelve little hourglasses in it and told the time by sand.

"It's almost twelve," she said. "Time to go out to the ball park. The game starts at one."

"Thanks," I said. "I'd forgotten about the time. When you started talking about President Roosevelt and waffles, my mind couldn't think of anything else. Two eggs. Those sound like great waffles. You'll have to make them for me sometime."

"Tonight, hero," she said. "Tonight."

I wished that tonight were here right now.

I wanted some waffles and to hear her talk some more about President Roosevelt.

Nebuchadnezzar

When we arrived at the ball park, there were
fifty thousand people waiting for me. They all stood up and
started cheering when they saw me come into the park.

Nebuchadnezzar had three extra units of cavalry there to
keep the fans under control. There had been a near riot the
day before and some people had been injured, so old "Neb"
was taking no chances with today's game.

The cavalry looked very smart in their armor.

I think they were glad to be at the ball game watching me
hit home runs. It certainly was a lot better than going to war.

I went down to the locker room and the girl went with
me. Her name was Nana-dirat. When I walked into the
locker room all the players stopped talking and watched as

I walked through and went into my own private dressing room. There was hushed silence. Nobody knew what to say. I don't blame them. After all, what do you say to somebody who has hit twenty-three home runs in their last twenty-three times at bat?

The team and I had gone far beyond small talk.

I was like a god to them.

They worshiped at the shrine of my bat.

The 596 B.C.
Baseball Season

The walls of my dressing room were covered with tapestries of my baseball feats woven in gold and covered with precious stones.

There was a tapestry of me beheading a pitcher with a line drive. Another tapestry showed a group of opposing players standing around a huge hole in the infield between second and third base. They never did find that ball. Still another tapestry showed me accepting a bowlful of jewels from Nebuchadnezzar for finishing the 596 B.C. season with an .890 batting average.

Nana-dirat took off my clothes and I lay down upon a solid gold dressing table and she gave me a pre-game massage with rare and exotic oils. Her hands were so gentle they felt like swans making love on a full moon night.

After massaging me Nana-dirat dressed me in my baseball uniform. It took her five minutes to put the uniform on. She did it very sensually. I had an erection by the time she finished with the uniform and I almost came when she put my shoes on. She ended by giving my spikes a delicate and loving caress.

Ah, paradise! There can be paradise on earth if you're a Babylonian baseball star.

First Base Hotel

"OK, asshole, wake up!" a voice came grinding into my ears like somebody deliberately stepping on an old lady's glasses. "You've had your beauty sleep! Wake up! This isn't a hotel! It's a baseball team!" the voice kept grinding.

My head felt as if a safe had dropped on it.

I opened my eyes and there was the manager and Sam standing above me, staring down. The manager really looked pissed off. Sam was smiling like a puppy with his buckteeth leading the way. I was lying on the grass beside first base.

The team was having batting practice. They kept looking over at me and making jokes. Everybody was having a good time except the manager and me.

"I knew you weren't a baseball player," he said. "You

don't look like a baseball player. I don't think you ever saw a baseball before."

"What happened?" I said.

"Listen to that, Sam," the manager said. "Did you get that? This punk asked me what happened. What in the fuck do you think happened? Run down the possibilities and then tell me what you think might have happened. What could have happened?" Then he started yelling again, "You got hit in the head! You just stood there like some kind of lamebrain and got hit in the head! You didn't even move! I don't think you even saw the baseball! You stood there like you were waiting to catch a bus!"

Then he reached down and grabbed me by the collar and started dragging me across the grass toward the street.

"Hey, stop it!" I said. "Stop it! My head is killing me. What are you doing?"

My words didn't have any effect on him. He just kept dragging me along. He left me lying out on the sidewalk. I lay there for a long time, first thinking that perhaps I wasn't cut out to be a professional baseball player. Then I thought about the dream I'd had of Babylon and how very pleasant it was.

Babylon . . . what a nice place.

That's how it started.

I've been going back ever since.

A Cowboy
in Babylon

Getting hit in the head with a baseball on June 20, 1933 was my ticket to Babylon. Anyway, I had a few hours to kill before I had to meet my first client in over three months, so I'd walked up from the morgue to Portsmouth Square on the edge of Chinatown and was sitting on a bench watching Chinese people come and go through the park.

Then I decided to do a little daydreaming about Babylon. I had everything under control: a loaded gun, some spare time, so I went to Babylon.

My latest adventures in Babylon concerned me having a big detective agency. I was the most famous private eye in Babylon. I had a fancy office just down from the Hanging Gardens. There were three very skillful operatives working for me and my secretary was a knockout, a real looker: Nana-dirat. She had become a permanent part of my adventures in Babylon. She was the perfect female counterpart for everything that I did there.

When I was a cowboy in Babylon, she was a school teacher who was kidnapped by the bad guys and I rescued her. We almost got married that time, but something came up, so it didn't happen.

During my military career when I was a general in Babylon, she was a nurse and nursed me back to health after I had suffered some terrible wounds in battle. She'd bathed my face with cool water as I lay suffering and delirious through hot nights in Babylon.

I just couldn't get enough of Nana-dirat.

She was always waiting for me in Babylon.

She of the long black hair and lissome body and breasts that were made to addle my senses. Just think: I never would have met her if I hadn't been hit in the head with a baseball.

Terry and the Pirates

Sometimes I played around with the form of
my adventures in Babylon. They would be done as books
that I could see in my mind what I was reading, but most
often they were done as movies, though once I did them as
a play with me being a Babylonian Hamlet and Nana-dirat
being both Gertrude and Ophelia. I abandoned the play
halfway through the second act. Someday I must return and
pick it up where I left off. It will have a different ending
from the way Shakespeare ended it. My *Hamlet* will have
a happy ending.

Nana-dirat and I will take off in an airplane of my own
invention built out of palm fronds and propelled by an
engine that burns honey. We will fly to Egypt to have

supper on a golden barge floating down the Nile with the Pharaoh.

Yes, I will have to pick that one up soon.

I had also done half-a-dozen adventures in Babylon in the form of comic strips. It was a lot of fun to do them that way. They were modelled after the style of *Terry and the Pirates*. Nana-dirat looked great as a comic-strip character.

I had just finished doing a private-eye mystery in detective magazine form like a short novel in *Dime Detective*. As I read the novel paragraph after paragraph, page following page, I translated the words into pictures that I could see and move rapidly forward in my mind like having a dream.

The mystery ended with me breaking the butler's arm as he tried to stab me with the same knife that he had used to murder the old dowager who'd been my client, having hired me to look into the matter of some stolen paintings.

"See," I said, turning triumphantly to Nana-dirat, leaving the murderous wretch to writhe in pain on the floor, the down payment for a life of thievery, betrayal and murder. "The butler did do it!"

"Ohhhhhhhhhh!" the butler moaned up from the floor.

"You didn't believe me," I said to Nana-dirat. "You said that the butler couldn't have done it, but I knew better and now the swine will pay for his crimes."

I gave him a good kick in the stomach. This caused him to stop concentrating on the pain in his arm and start thinking about his stomach.

Not only was I the most famous detective in Babylon but I was also the most hard-boiled just like a rock. I had no use for lawbreakers and could be very brutal with them.

"Darling," Nana-dirat said. "You're so wonderful, but did you have to kick him in the stomach?"

"Yes," I said.

Nana-dirat threw her arms around me and pressed her beautiful body up close to mine. Then she looked up into my cold steel eyes and smiled. "Oh, well," she said. "Nobody's perfect, you big lug."

"Mercy," the butler said.

Case closed!

Ming the Merciless

       Sitting there on the park bench with the United States of America freshly at war with Japan, Germany and Italy, I decided to do my next adventure as a private eye in Babylon in the form of a serial that would have fifteen chapters.

I of course would be the hero and Nana-dirat the heroine, my faithful and loving secretary. I decided to borrow Ming the Merciless from *Flash Gordon* to be the villain.

I had to change his name and alter his character slightly to fit my needs. That wouldn't be hard. Actually, it would be an immense amount of pleasure for me. I had spent a very pleasant part of eight years making up situations and characters in Babylon, unfortunately to the point of being a detriment to my real life, such as it was.

I'd much rather be in ancient Babylon than in the Twentieth Century trying to put two bits together for a hamburger and I love Nana-dirat more than any woman I've ever met in the flesh.

First, what to do with Ming the Merciless? Change his name. That was the first thing that had to be done. In my serial he would be Dr. Abdul Forsythe, publicly known as one of the most generous and kindest men in Babylon but secretly he had a laboratory under the clinic that he used to provide free medical services for the poor. In the laboratory he was constructing a powerful and evil ray that he was going to conquer the world with.

The ray changed people into shadow robots that were totally subservient to Dr. Forsythe and would do his evil work, responding to his slightest beckoning.

He had a plan for creating artificial night composed of his shadow robots that would move during the real night from town to town conquering unsuspecting citizens and changing them into more shadow robots.

It was an ingenious plan and he had already changed thousands of unsuspecting and helpless poor people that came to his clinic seeking free medical help into shadow robots.

They came to be helped by Dr. Forsythe and then disappeared from the face of the earth. Their absence was hardly noticed in Babylon because they were poor. Sometimes relatives or friends would come by and inquire into their disappearance. Often, they, too, would disappear.

63

The fiend!

He needed only one more ingredient to put his plan into action. After he changed them into shadow robots, he stacked them like newspapers in a hidden warehouse nearby, waiting for the time to come when he could turn them loose on the world as artificial night.

The Magician

Escitybrell. Escitybrell.

I heard a sound in the distance that was directed toward me but I couldn't make it out.

"Excuse me. Excuse me."

The sound was words.

Babylon fell over on its side and lay there.

"Excuse me, C. Card, is that you?"

I looked up, totally returned to the so-called real world. The voice belonged to an old comrade in arms from the Spanish Civil War. I hadn't seen him in years.

"Well, I'll be," I said. "Sam Herschberger. Those nights in Madrid. Those were the days."

I stood up and we shook hands. I had to shake his left

hand because his right hand wasn't there. I remembered when he'd gotten it blown off. It had not been a good day for him because he was a professional juggler and magician. When he looked at his blown-off hand lying on the ground nearby, all he could say was, "This is one trick I'll never be able to duplicate."

"You seemed a million miles away," he said, now years later in San Francisco.

"I was daydreaming," I said.

"Just like the good old days," he said. "I think half the time I knew you in Spain you weren't even there."

I decided to change the subject.

"What are you up to these days?" I said.

"I'm working just as much as all the other one-armed jugglers and magicians are."

"That bad, huh?"

"No, I can't complain. I married a woman who owns a beauty parlor and she's got a thing for people with missing limbs. Sometimes she hints that I would be twice as sexy as I am now if I only had one leg, but that's the way it goes. It beats working for a living."

"What about the Party?" I said. "I thought they loved you."

"With two arms they loved me," he said. "I wasn't much use to them with only one. They used me as a warm-up act for recruiting farm workers over in the valley. They'd gather around to watch me juggle and do tricks and then they'd hear about Karl Marx and how great Soviet Russia was and Lenin. Oh, well, that was a long time ago. A guy's got to keep moving. If you don't the grass will grow on you. What have you been doing? The last time I saw you, you had a couple of bullet holes in your ass and you were going to be a doctor. How'd you get shot in the ass, anyway? As I remember the Fascists were on our left flank and there was nobody behind us and you were in a trench. Where did the bullets come from that got you? That's always been a mystery to me."

I wasn't going to tell him that I slipped while I was taking a shit and sat down on my pistol causing it to go off and blow a couple of holes clean through both cheeks of my ass.

"Water under the bridge," I said. "It hurts just to think about it."

"I know what you mean," he said, looking down at the place where his right hand used to be.

"Anyway, did you become a doctor?"

"No," I said. "That didn't work out the way I planned it."

"What are you doing, then?"

"I'm a private eye," I said.

"A private eye?" he said.

Barcelona

The last time I'd seen Sam had been in Barcelona in '38. He had been a hell-of-a-good juggler and magician. Too bad about his arm, but it sounded to me as if he was using its absence to best advantage. A guy's got to make do.

We shared some Spanish Civil War memories and then I hit him up for five bucks. I try not to let a chance go by.

"By the way," I said. "Did you ever repay me that five you borrowed in Barcelona?"

"What five?" he said.

"You don't remember?" I said.

"No," he said.

"Then forget it," I said. "No big deal." Then I started to change the subject—

"Wait a minute," he said. He had always been an unscrupulously honest person. "I don't remember borrowing five dollars from you. When was that?"

"In Barcelona. A week before we left, but forget it. It's OK. If you don't remember it, I don't want to bring it up. It's the past. Forget it," and I started to change the subject again.

A few moments later, after he had given me the five bucks, with a curious expression on his face he walked up Washington Street and out of my life.

The Abraham Lincoln Brigade

The Spanish Civil War was a long way off but I was glad that it was able to yield five dollars years later. I hadn't really been a political enthusiast. That wasn't the reason that I joined the Abraham Lincoln Brigade. I went to Spain because I thought it might resemble Babylon. I don't know where I got that idea. I get a lot of ideas about Babylon. Some of them are right on the money and others are half-baked. The only trouble is that it's hard to tell which are which, but it always works itself out in the end. Anyway, it does for me when I'm dreaming of Babylon.

Then I remembered that I still had to make that phone call, but for a few seconds I didn't know whether I was supposed to call Babylon or my mother out in the Mission District.

It was my mother.

I promised her a call and I knew that she'd be upset if I didn't call her soon, though we didn't have anything to talk about because we couldn't stand each other and always got into the same arguments.

She didn't like the idea of me being a private eye.

Yes, I'd better call Mom. She'd be angrier than she normally was if I didn't call her today. I hated to do it but if I didn't I'd have hell to pay for it. I called her once a week and we always had the same conversation. I don't think we even bothered to change the words. I think we used the same words all the time.

It would go just like this:

"Hello?" my mother would say when she answered the telephone.

"Hi, Mom. It's me."

"Hello? who is this speaking? Hello?"

"Mom."

"This can't be my son calling. Hello?"

"Mom," I'd always whine.

"It sounds like my son," she'd always say. "But he wouldn't have the nerve to call if he was still a private detective. He just wouldn't have the nerve. He still has some self-respect left. If this is my son, then he must have given up his private-eye nonsense and now he has a decent job. He's a working stiff who can hold his head up high and he wants to pay back the eight hundred dollars that he owes his mother. Good boy."

Then after she finished speaking, there would always be a long pause and I'd say, "This is your son and I'm still a private detective. I've got a case. I'm going to pay back some of the money I owe you soon."

I'd always tell her that I had a case even if I didn't have one. It was part of the routine.

"You've broken your mother's heart," she'd always say then and I'd answer, "Don't say that, Mom, just because I'm a private detective. I still love you."

"What about the eight hundred dollars?" she'd say. "My son's love can't pay for a quart of milk or a loaf of bread. Who do you think you are, anyway? Breaking my heart. Never having a decent job. Owing me eight hundred dollars. Being a private detective. Never getting married. No grandchildren. What am I going to do? Why did I have to be cursed with a son who is an idiot?"

"*Mom,* don't say things like that," I'd whine on cue. That whining used to be able to spring a five spot or ten dollars out of her but nothing these days, nothing at all. It was just plain whining but if I didn't call her it made things worse, so I'd call her because I didn't want things to get any worse than what they were.

My father died years ago.

My mother still hadn't gotten over it.

"Your poor father," she'd say and then would start crying. "It's your fault that I'm a widow."

My mother blamed me for my father's death and in a way it was my fault, even if I was only four years old at the time. She'd always bring it up on the telephone. "Brat!" she'd yell. "Evil brat!"

"*Mom,*" I'd whine.

Then she'd stop crying and say, "I shouldn't blame you. You were only four at the time. It's not your fault. But why did you have to throw your ball out in the street? Why couldn't you have just bounced it on the sidewalk like any other kid who still has a father?"

"You know I'm sorry, Mom."

"I know you're sorry, son, but why are you a private detective? I hate those magazines and books. They're so seamy. I don't like the long black shadows those people have on the covers. They frighten me."

"Those aren't the real thing, Mom," I'd always say, and she'd answer, "Then why do they sell them at the newsstand for everyone in the world to see and buy. Answer that one if you can, Smart Guy. Come on and answer it, Mr. Private Eye. I dare you. Come on! Come on! This is your mother!"

I couldn't answer it.

I couldn't tell my mother that people wanted to read stories about people who had long black ominous shadows. She just wouldn't have understood. Her thinking didn't run along those lines.

She would end the conversation by saying, "Son . . . ," pausing for a long time, ". . . why a private detective?"

We'd been having the same conversation now for six months.

I sure wish I hadn't run out of money, trying to be a private detective and had to borrow so much from my mother and all my friends.

Well, anyway, my luck was going to turn today.

I had a client and some bullets for my gun.

Everything was going to turn out OK in the end.

That's what counts.

It would be a turning point.

I'd get lots of clients, pay back all my debts, have an office, a secretary and a car again, but this time I would have a secretary that would fuck my ears off. Then I'd take a vacation to Mexico and just sit there on the beach, dreaming of Babylon. Nana-dirat would be right beside me, looking great in a bathing suit, but right now I'd better call my mother.

Loving Uncle Sam

I went into a nearby bar on Kearny Street to use their pay telephone. The place was empty except for the bartender and a fat lady who was on the phone. She wasn't talking. She was just standing there, nodding her head to the person on the other end of the line.

I decided to have a quick beer from my new five dollar bill while she finished her call. I sat down on a stool and the bartender walked down the bar to me. He was so ordinary looking that he was almost invisible.

"What will you have?" he said.

"Just a beer," I said.

"Better drink it in a hurry," the bartender said. "The

Japanese might be here by dark." Somehow he thought that this was very funny and laughed heartily at his "joke."

"The Japanese love beer," he said, continuing to laugh. "They're going to drink every drop in California when they get here."

I looked over at the fat lady nodding her head up and down like a duck. There was a huge smile on her face. She looked as if she were at the beginning of a telephone conversation that might take years to finish.

"Forget the beer," I said to the bartender and got up from my stool and headed toward the door. I hadn't had a beer in weeks and I didn't want it ruined by a bartender who didn't make any sense.

I think he had a few nuts and bolts loose in his head. No wonder the bar was empty except for the fat woman who was having a love affair with a pay phone.

I now pronounce you telephone and wife.

"Every drop," the bartender laughed as I went through the door and back out onto Kearny Street, almost knocking a Chinaman over as I stepped outside. He was walking by on the street and I stepped through the door right into him. We were both very surprised but he was more surprised than I was.

He had a package under his arm when we collided. He juggled it briefly and managed to keep it from falling on the sidewalk. He was very ruffled by the incident.

"Not Japanese," he said, turning to me as he started to hurry away. "Chinese-American. Love flag. Love Uncle Sam. No trouble. Chinese. Not Japanese. Loyal. Pay taxes. Keep nose clean."

Bus Throne

Things were starting to get too complicated. I'd better call my mother later on when things got a little simpler. I didn't want to push my luck while I was ahead of the game, so I decided to go home and take a shower before I met my client.

Maybe I had a shirt that resembled something clean in the closet. I wanted to look my best for my client. I'd even brush my teeth.

I walked down Kearny to Sacramento Street and waited for the bus to take me up Sacramento to Nob Hill and my apartment. I didn't have to wait long. The bus was only a few blocks away coming up Sacramento toward my stop.

See: Luck was running my way.

I think that luck is like the tide.

When it comes in, it comes in.

I was really going to enjoy the luxury of the bus trip. I had been hoofing it around San Francisco for weeks. This was the poorest I'd ever been but those days were over now.

I got onto the bus, paid my nickel and sat down as if I were a king enjoying a brand-new throne. I sighed with pleasure as the bus started up Sacramento. I think I sighed a little too loudly because a young woman who was sitting with her legs crossed in a seat opposite me, uncrossed her legs and turned her head uncomfortably the other way.

She'd probably had a bus seat every God-damn day of her life. She may even have been born on a bus and had a lifetime ticket, and when she died, they'd take her coffin on a bus to the cemetery. It would be painted black of course and all the seats filled with flowers like crazy passengers.

Some people don't appreciate how good they've got it.

Drums of
Fu Manchu

The short trip on the bus up the hill was a
good time to do a little thinking about my private-eye serial
in Babylon. I settled back and Babylon took over my mind
like warm maple syrup being poured over piping hot pan-
cakes.

. . . ummmmm good.

. . . ummmmm Babylon.

I had to have a name for my serial.

What was I going to call it?

Let's see.

Then I thought about the names of serials I'd seen in the
last few years. I'm really quite a movie fan:

Mandrake the Magician
The Phantom Creeps
Adventures of Captain Marvel
Mysterious Dr. Satan
The Shadow
Drums of Fu Manchu
and The Iron Claw.

Those were all good titles and I needed one just as good for my serial. As the bus travelled toward the top of Nob Hill, stopping and starting, picking up passengers and letting passengers off, I ran a hundred titles through my mind. The best ones I came up with were:

The Horror of Dr. Abdul Forsythe
Adventures of a Private Eye in Babylon
The Shadow Robots Creep.

Yes, this was going to be fun. I had a lot of possibilities to work with, but I had to be careful not to let things run away with themselves. Even with a tight rein on Babylon, I still went two stops past my stop and had to walk back a couple of blocks.

I had to watch myself very carefully, especially because I had a client, not to let Babylon get the best of me again.

Friday's Grave

I saw a pay telephone.

Maybe I'd better call my mother and get it over with. The sooner I called her, the sooner I wouldn't have to call her again. It would be taken care of for another week.

I dropped a nickel in the slot and dialed.

I let the phone ring ten times before I hung up.

I wondered where she was.

Then I remembered that it was Friday and she was at the cemetery putting flowers on my father's grave. She did that every Friday. It was a ritual with her, rain or shine, she visited his grave every Friday.

Maybe today wasn't the day to call her.

It would only remind her that I had killed him when I was four years old.

No, I'd better call tomorrow.

That would be a smart move on my part.

I started to think about the day I killed my father. I got as far as remembering that it was a Sunday and a very warm day and a brand-new Model T sedan was parked in the street in front of our house and I had walked over to it earlier and had smelled how new the car was. I was a kid then and just walked right over and put my nose directly down on a fender and gave it a big sniff.

I think the best perfume in this world is the smell of something brand-new. It can be clothes or furniture or radios or cars, even appliances like toasters or electric irons. They all smell good to me when they're brand-new.

Anyway, I was remembering back to the morning that I killed my father. I had gotten as far as having my nose on the fender of a brand-new Model T when I suddenly rerouted my thinking. I didn't want to think about killing my father, so I just changed the subject in my mind.

I couldn't think about Babylon or I might blow it, so I thought about my client.

Who was my client?

What did they look like?

What did they want done?

Why did I have to have a gun?

Were they going to ask me to do something illegal?

If they did, of course, I would do it, short of killing somebody. Beggars can't be choosers. A man in my boat has to row where he's told to except that I wasn't going to kill anybody. That was the only thing I wouldn't do. I was really desperate. I needed the God-damn money.

I didn't know whether my client was a man or a woman. All I knew was that I was supposed to meet somebody in front of a radio station at 6 P.M. They already knew what I looked like, so I didn't have to know what they looked like. It only made sense if you were as broke as I was, and it made a lot of sense to me.

Smith

Thinking about the fact that I didn't know the name or sex of my client somehow returned me to Babylon and my serial.

Sometimes Babylon just happens like that.

What was I doing trying to think up a title for the serial when I hadn't even given all my main characters names yet? There was of course a name for the villain: Dr. Abdul Forsythe, but I didn't even have a name for myself.

Oh, boy, where was my noggin? I'd better get a name for me. I might want to use it in the title.

I had used the name Ace Stag for my name in the detective novel about Babylon that I had just finished living, but I didn't like to use the same name for myself in my Babylonian adventures. I liked to change my name. For instance, when I was a baseball hero in Babylon, I used the name Samson Ruth, but enough of that. I needed a new name for myself in the serial.

I tried out a few names as I backtracked the two blocks to my intended bus stop. I like the name Smith. I don't know why but I've always liked that name. Some people consider it ordinary. I don't.

Smith . . .

I ran some variations of Smith through my mind:

Errol Smith

Cary Smith

Humphrey Smith

George Smith (as in Raft)

Wallace Smith

Pancho Smith

Lee Smith

Morgan Smith

"Gunboat" Smith

"Red" Smith

Carter Smith

Rex Smith

Cody Smith

Flint Smith

Terry Smith

Laughing Smith

Major Smith (I liked that one a lot.)

"Oklahoma Jimmy" Smith

F.D.R. Smith

There certainly are a lot of possibilities when you use the name Smith.

Some of the names were good but so far I hadn't come up with one that was perfect and I wouldn't settle for less than a perfect Smith.

Why should I?

Lobotomy

Ah, shit!

I walked two blocks beyond my stop the other way, past the street that I lived on, thinking about having the name Smith for a private eye in Babylon, so I had to turn around and walk back again and felt like a fool because I couldn't afford to do things like that when I was just a few hours away from my first client in months.

Thinking about Babylon can be a dangerous thing for me.

I had to watch my ass.

I walked back down Sacramento Street *very* carefully not thinking about Babylon. As I walked along, I pretended that I had a prefrontal lobotomy.

The Milkmen

I felt a certain sense of triumph when I arrived at Leavenworth Street and walked half a block to the broken-down apartment building I was living in. I hadn't thought about Babylon once.

The morgue wagon was parked in front of the apartment house. Somebody had died in the building. I tried to imagine one of the tenants being dead but I couldn't imagine anyone being dead in that place. Why bother when paying your rent there was a form of death?

I certainly was going to be surprised when I found out who it was.

The morgue wagon was a converted panel Mack truck

with enough corpse room to accommodate four brand-new ex-taxpayers.

I walked up the steps and opened the front door and stepped into the dark musty hall of the building that some called home but I called shit.

Though I had cooled the rent business with the landlady, I involuntarily looked up the stairs to the second floor and her apartment. The door was open and two morgue attendants were carrying her body out. It was lying on a stretcher covered with a sheet. There were some tenants cluttered around the door. They acted like amateur, just-drafted mourners.

I stood at the bottom of the landing and watched the attendants bring her body down the stairs. They did it very smoothly, almost effortlessly, like olive oil pouring out of a bottle.

They didn't say anything as they came down the stairs. I knew a lot of guys who worked at the morgue but I didn't know these guys.

The tenant mourners stood in a very small crowd at the top of the stairs whispering and mourning amateurishly. They weren't very good at it. Of course how good can you be at mourning a landlady who had a shrill temper and was a big snoop? She had a bad habit of peeking out a crack in the door to her apartment and scrutinizing everybody who came and went in the building. She had incredible hearing. I think there was a bat somewhere in her family tree.

Well, those days were over for her.

She was now taking a trip down to my peg-legged friend who'd be putting her on ice shortly. I wondered if he would do any sight-seeing on her naked body. No, I don't think so. She was too old and had eaten too many stale doughnuts. She couldn't hold a candle to that prostitute who was keeping him company now, the one who'd been opened up with a letter opener.

For a few seconds, I saw her dead body in my mind. She was a real looker. Then I thought about the beautiful blonde that I'd met leaving the morgue and how she'd been crying when I saw her but had pretended to be very aloof and distant to Peg-leg when she'd looked at the body of the dead whore. That line of thought led to a flash of her chauffeur smiling at me as they drove away up the street, almost as if he knew me, that we were old friends who didn't have time to talk right now but we'd see each other soon.

I mentally returned to the business at hand, watching the attendants complete getting the dead landlady's body down the stairs. They sure were good at it. Of course that was their occupation but I had to admire it. I think there's an art to doing everything and they were proving my theory by moving that old bag's carcass just like she was an angel or at least a millionaire.

"The landlady?" I said as they finished getting her down the stairs. Saying that made me sound like a private detective. I like to keep in shape.

"Yup," one of them said.

"What was it?" I said.

"Ticker," the other one said.

The amateur mourners followed down the stairs and watched the attendants finish carting her out of the building. They slid her body into the back of the morgue wagon. There was already another corpse in there, so she'd have some company on her trip downtown to the morgue. I guess it beats going by yourself.

The attendants closed the door behind her and her new-found friend. They walked slowly around and got into the front seat. There was a very offhand casualness to their demeanor. They had about the same attitude toward dead bodies as a milkman does toward empty bottles. You just pick them up and take them away.

My Day

After the landlady was gone I walked down the hall to my apartment and suddenly the bright side of the situation came into focus. The old landlady owned the building and she was a widow and she didn't have any relatives or friends. Her estate would be in a complete mess. It would take months to sort out, so nobody would be bothering me about my overdue rent.

What a break!

This was really my day.

I hadn't had a day like this since that car ran over me a couple years ago and broke both my legs. I got a nice settlement out of that. Even though I was in traction for three months, it beat working for a living and oh, what times I had! dreaming of Babylon there in the hospital.

I almost hated to leave.

I guess I showed it.

The nurses made some jokes about it.

"Why so gloomy?" one of them said.

"You look as if you're going to a funeral," another one said.

They didn't know how comfortable the hospital was, just to lie there and have all my wants taken care of, with practically nothing to do except dream of Babylon.

The second I went out the front door of that hospital on my crutches everything started downhill. From then on it just kept spiralling down until today, and what a day it had been so far: a client! Bullets for my gun! Five dollars! And best of all, a dead landlady!

Who could ask for anything more?

Christmas Carols

The dank grubbiness of my apartment hadn't changed while I was gone. What a rock bottom hole . . . Jesus, how could I live the way I was living? It was a little frightening. I stepped over some unidentified objects lying on the floor. I deliberately didn't look at them very hard. I didn't want to know what they were. I also avoided looking at my bed.

My bed resembled something that belonged in the violent ward of an insane asylum. I had never really been much of a bedmaker even when I had been inspired to do so in days long gone past.

My mother used to yell at me all the time, "Why don't

you make your bed! Do I have to do everything for you!"

After I made my bed, she'd yell, "Why can't you make your bed right! Look at those sheets! They look like nooses. I don't know what I'm going to do! Mercy, Lord, please mercy!" And now I owed her eight hundred dollars and my bed looked like the gallows they hanged the people who'd assassinated Abraham Lincoln from, and I hadn't called my mother this week.

I needed a shower to impress my client, so I took my clothes off and was just about to turn the shower on when I realized that I didn't have any soap. I'd used up the last little scrap a few days before. Also, my razor possessed a blade so dull that you couldn't shave a pear with it.

I thought about putting my clothes back on and going out and getting some soap and some razor blades, but then I remembered that there wasn't a store within a mile of the place that I didn't owe money to. If I flashed that five dollar bill in front of a store owner, he'd tear me limb from limb.

No, sir . . .

What was I to do?

I couldn't borrow some soap or a razor blade from any of the tenants in the building because there wasn't a single one that I hadn't borrowed down like a forest fire. They wouldn't loan me a Band-Aid if my throat was cut.

I thought it all over very carefully.

My thinking went something like this: Water is more important than soap. I mean, what is soap without water? Nothing. That's what it is. So logically water could handle the situation by itself, and also it was better than nothing, if you know what I mean.

Having convinced myself of this logic, I turned the water on and stepped into the shower. I immediately stepped back out.

"YEOWWWWWWWWWWWWWWWWWW!" I yelled, jumping around in agony.

The water had been scalding hot and I was paying for it. Too bad my thinking had not been carried to the point of adjusting the temperature of the water so that a human being could stand it.

Oh, well . . .

It was just an oversight on my part. As soon as the pain stopped, I adjusted the hot and cold faucets so that they combined to create an acceptable environment for a shower without soap.

Normally, I sing in the shower, so I started singing in the shower:

"O come, all ye faithful, Joyful and triumphant,
O come ye, O come ye to Bethlehem.
Come and behold Him, Born the King of angels . . ."

I always sing Christmas carols in the shower.

A few years ago a woman spent the night with me when I was living in a fancier apartment. She was the secretary to a used-car dealer. I really liked her. I had hopes that we might get something heavy going between us and maybe a few bucks off a used car.

We'd gone out on a few dates together but this was our first time together in bed and we did pretty good at it, anyway, I thought so. Those were the days when I had soap, so in the morning I went in to take a shower. She was still lying in bed when I left the room. I got into the shower and started singing:

"It came upon a midnight clear that glorious song of old . . ."

I sang away . . .

When I finished my shower I returned to the bedroom and she was gone. She'd gotten up, dressed and left without saying a word, but she'd left a note on the table beside my bed.

The note read:

Dear Mr. Card,

Thanks for a nice time. Please don't call me again.

Yours sincerely,
Dottie Jones

I guess some people don't want to hear Christmas carols in July.

A World Renowned Expert on Socks

I finished my personal hygienic orgy by throwing the world's least effective shave on my face, thanks to the dullness of the razor blade, the sharpest one I had.

Then I sorted through various piles of my clothes and put together the cleanest wardrobe I could under the conditions brought about by months of extreme poverty, and also I made sure that I had two socks on. They of course didn't match but they were close enough, not unless you were a world renowned expert on socks.

Thank God all of that was going to be taken care of by my new client. They'd get me out of this hell I was in.

I looked over at the clock on the table beside my bed.

Its face barely peeked out from a thousand bits of hope-less clutter. The clock didn't look too happy. I think it would have preferred to have been in the house of a banker or a spinster schoolteacher instead of a San Francisco private eye down on his luck. The hands of the de-moralized clock said 5:15. I had forty-five minutes before I was to meet my client in front of the radio station on Powell Street.

I hoped that whatever my client wanted me to do would take place in the radio station because I'd never been in a radio station before and I liked to listen to the radio. I had a lot of favorite programs.

Well, now I was "showered," "shaved," "clean," and "clothed." It was about time I headed downtown. I decided to walk because I was so used to it, but those days were over. My client's fat fee would end that routine, so this walk downtown was a sort of farewell to walking all over the place.

I put the coat back on that had a gun in each pocket: one loaded and one empty. Looking back on it now, I wish I had taken the empty gun out of my pocket, but you can't go back and redo the past. You just have to live with it.

Before leaving the apartment I looked around to see if I had forgotten anything. I of course hadn't. I had so little stuff in this world what in the hell did I have to for-get?

A watch, no, a signet ring with a huge diamond, no, a good-luck rabbit's foot, nope. I had eaten that long ago. So just standing there with the two guns in my pockets, I was as ready to leave as I was ever going to be.

The only thing that was nagging my mind was the fact that I still had to call my mother and have the same conversation all over again and take my week's abuse.

Oh, well . . . if they wanted life to be perfect they would have made it that way in the first place and I'm not talking about the Garden of Eden.

Good-bye, Oil Wells in Rhode Island

The amateur landlady mourners were not at the top of the stairs when I left the building. They certainly had been a ridiculous crew drafted into a pathetic opera of mourning, but now they had all gone back to their ratholes and the landlady was only dead.

I thought about her as I left the place.

I had certainly done a good con job on her when I had gotten a reprieve on my rent by telling her that my uncle had struck it rich with oil wells in Rhode Island. That was a great inspiration, right out of left field, and she bought it. I could have been a great politician if Babylon hadn't gotten in my way.

As I went down the front stairs, I had a vision of the

landlady thinking about oil wells in Rhode Island just as her ticker stopped. I could hear her saying outloud to herself, "I never heard of oil wells in Rhode Island before. Somehow that doesn't sound right to me. I know there are a lot of oil wells in Oklahoma and Texas, and I've seen them in Southern California, but oil wells in Rhode Island?"

Then her heart stopped.

Good.

Pretty Pictures

I was walking down Leavenworth Street, very carefully not thinking about Babylon, when suddenly a young man in his early twenties spotted me from across the street and started waving his arms at me.

I had never seen him before.

I didn't know who he was.

I wondered what was up.

He was very anxious to get across the street to me but the light was red and he stood there waiting for it to change. While he waited he kept waving his arms in the air like a crazy windmill.

When the light changed he ran across the street to me.

"Hello, hello," he said like a long-lost brother.

His face was covered with acne and his eyes suffered from character weakness. Who was this bozo?

"Do you remember me?" he said.

I didn't and even if I did, I didn't want to, but as I said I didn't.

"No, I don't remember you," I said.

His clothes were a mess.

He looked as bad as I did.

When I said that I didn't know him, he looked very disheartened as if we had been very good friends and I had forgotten all about him.

Where in the hell did this guy come from?

He was now staring at his feet like a freshly-disciplined puppy.

"Who are you?" I said.

"You don't remember me," he said, sadly.

"Tell me who you are and maybe I'll remember you," I said.

He was now shaking his head dejectedly.

"Well, come on," I said. "Spill the beans. Who are you?"

He continued shaking his head.

I started to walk past him.

He reached out and touched my coat with his hand, so as to stop me from walking away. That gave me two reasons now to have my coat cleaned.

"You sold me some pictures," he said, slowly.

"Pictures?" I said.

"Yeah, pictures of lady women with no clothes on. They were pretty pictures. I took them home. Remember Treasure Island? The Worlds Fair? I took the pictures home with me."

Oh, shit! I bet he took the pictures home with him.

"I need some more pictures," he said. "Those pictures are old."

I had a vision of what those pictures looked like now and shuddered.

"Do you have some more I can buy?" he said. "I need new pictures."

"That was a long time ago," I said. "I'm not doing that any more. That was just a one-time thing."

"No, it was 1940," he said. "That was only two years ago. Don't you have just a few left over? I'll pay you good for them."

He was now staring at me with dog-like pleading eyes. He was desperate for pornography. I'd seen that look before, but those days of selling dirty pictures were behind me now.

"Fuck you, pervert!" I said and continued on down Leavenworth Street toward the radio station.

I had better things to do than stand on a street corner talking to asshole sex perverts. I shuddered again thinking about how those pictures I sold him at the Worlds Fair in 1940 got old.

Pedro and
His Five Romantics

        I walked a few more blocks down Leavenworth
Street toward meeting my client and then remembered the
dream I'd had last night. I dreamt that I was a famous chef
from South of the Border and I opened up a Mexican
restaurant in Babylon specializing in chiles rellenos and
cheese enchiladas.

It became the most famous restaurant in Babylon.

It was near the Hanging Gardens and the finest people
in Babylon ate there. Nebuchadnezzar came there often,
but he didn't care for the house specialties. He preferred
tacos. Sometimes he would be sitting there with one in each
hand.

What a character, making jokes all the time and gesturing at people with his tacos.

Nana-dirat worked there as a dancer.

The place had a stage with a small mariachi band: Pedro and His Five Romantics.

They could play up a storm and when Nana-dirat danced everybody ordered more beer to cool themselves off. She was a Mexican firecracker dancing in old Babylon.

Uh-oh, suddenly I realized as I was walking down the street toward my client that I was thinking about Babylon again. Big mistake.

I stopped it immediately.

I slammed on the brakes.

Got to be careful. Can't let Babylon get me. I had too many things going for me. Later for Babylon. So I rearranged my thought patterns to concentrate on something else and the thing I chose to think about was my shoes. I needed a new pair. The ones I was wearing were worn out.

Smith Smith

I was a block away from the radio station, busy thinking about my shoes, when the name Smith Smith flashed into my mind and I blurted out, "Great!" The whole world could have heard me but fortunately there was nobody around. That block of Powell Street was quiet. There were a few people at each end of the block but I was alone in the middle of the block.

Luck was still with me.

Smith Smith, I thought, *that's the name for my private eye in Babylon.* He'll be called Smith Smith.

I'd come up with the perfect variation of the name Smith. I'd combined it with a second Smith. I was really proud of myself. Too bad I didn't have anybody to share my accomplishment with but I knew if I told anybody about Smith Smith it would be good cause for an involuntary trip to the nuthouse, which was where I wasn't interested in going.

I'd keep Smith Smith to myself.

I went back to thinking about my shoes.

Roast Turkey
and Dressing

I arrived at the radio station at ten of six. I wanted to be on time to show that I was a responsible private detective who had better things to do than think about Babylon all the time.

There was nobody else in front of the radio station.

My client whoever they were hadn't arrived yet.

I was very curious about who would show up.

I didn't know whether it would be a man or a woman. If it was a woman I hoped that she would be very rich and beautiful and she would fall madly in love with me and want me to retire from the private-eye business and live a life of luxury, and I'd spend half my time fucking her, the other half dreaming of Babylon.

It would be a good life.

I could hardly wait to get started.

Then I thought about what would happen if a Sydney Greenstreet–type client showed up who wanted me to tail a Filipino cook who was having a love affair with his wife, and I'd have to spend a lot of time sitting at the counter of the café that he cooked in, watching him cook.

The case would take a month.

Every week I'd meet with Sydney Greenstreet in his huge Pacific Heights apartment and describe in detail to him everything the Filipino cook had done that week. He was very interested in everything the Filipino cook did, even to the point of wanting to know what the menu was on Wednesday in the restaurant the cook worked at.

I'd be sitting opposite Sydney Greenstreet in this fantastic apartment filled with rare art works. The apartment would have a tremendous view of San Francisco, and I'd have a glass of fifty-year-old sherry in my hand that was constantly being refilled by Peter Lorre who was the butler.

Peter Lorre would project an illusion of poised disinterest in our conversation when he was in the room with us, but later I would see him hovering near the door to the room, eavesdropping.

"What was the menu on Wednesday?" Sydney Greenstreet would say with his huge fleshy hand incongruously wrapped around a delicate sherry glass.

Peter Lorre would be hovering on the other side of the open living room door, pretending that he was dusting a large vase but actually listening very carefully to what we were saying.

"The soup was rice tomato," I'd say. "The salad was a Waldorf salad."

"I'm not interested in the soup," Sydney Greenstreet would say. "Or the salad. I want to know what the entrées were."

"I'm sorry," I'd say. After all, it was his money. He was paying the bill. "The entrées were:

Fried Prawns
Grilled Sea Bass with Lemon Butter
Filet of Sole with Tartar Sauce
Veal Fricassee with Vegetables
Corned Beef Hash with Egg
Grilled Pork Chop and Apple Sauce
Grilled Baby Beef Liver and Onions
Chicken Croquettes
Ham Croquettes with Pineapple Sauce
Breaded Veal Cutlet with Brown Sauce
Fried Unjointed Spring Chicken
Baked Virginia Ham with Sweet Potatoes
Roast Turkey and Dressing
Corn-fed Steer Beef Club Sirloin Steak
French Lamb Chops and Green Peas
New York Cut Sirloin."

"Did you try one of the entrées?" he'd ask.

"Yes," I'd say. "I had the roast turkey and dressing."

"How was it?" he would ask, leaning anxiously toward me in his chair.

"Terrible," I'd say.

"Good," he'd say, with a great deal of relish, smacking his

lips with pleasure. "I don't understand what she sees in him. They're both swine. They deserve each other."

Then he would pause and lean back comfortably in his chair and take an appreciative sip of sherry. He would look at me with contentment in his lazy tropical eyes.

"The roast turkey and dressing were terrible?" he'd ask. "Were they really that bad?" with almost a smile on his face.

"The dressing was the worst I ever tasted," I'd say. "I think it was made out of dog shit. I don't know how anyone could eat it. I took one taste and that was enough for me."

"How interesting," Sydney Greenstreet would say. "How very interesting."

I'd look over at Peter Lorre who'd be pretending to dust a large green vase with Chinamen riding horses on it.

He would also think my comments on the roast turkey and dressing were interesting, too.

Cinderella
of the Airways

I was standing there in front of radio station WXYZ "Cinderella of the Airways" thinking about Sydney Greenstreet and Peter Lorre, roast turkey and dressing, when the Cadillac limousine that had driven by me earlier in the day when I was going into the morgue pulled up in front of me and the rear door opened effortlessly toward me. The beautiful blonde I'd seen leaving the morgue was sitting in the back seat of the limousine.

She gestured with her eyes for me to get in.

It was a blue gesture.

I got in beside her.

She was wearing a fur coat that was worth more than all

the people I know put together and multiplied twice. She smiled. "What a coincidence," she said. "We saw each other at the morgue. It's a small world."

"It sure is," I said. "I take it that you're my—"

"Client," she said. "Do you have a gun?"

"Yes," I said. "I've got one."

"Good," she said. "That's very good. I think we're going to be friends. Close friends."

"Why do you need somebody with a gun? What am I supposed to do?" I said.

"I've seen all the movies," she said, smiling. She had perfect teeth. They were so perfect that they made me feel self-conscious about my teeth. I felt as if I had a mouth full of broken glass.

The same chauffeur who'd been driving her earlier in the day was in the front seat behind the wheel. He had a very powerful-looking neck. He hadn't looked back once since I'd gotten into the car. He just kept staring straight ahead. His neck looked as if it could dent an ax.

"Cozy?" the rich blonde said.

"Sure," I said, having seen this movie before.

"Mr. Cleveland," she said, addressing the chauffeur who answered her with a twitch of his neck.

The car started slowly down the street.

"Where are we off to?" I said, offhandedly.

"Sausalito to have a beer," she said.

That seemed strange.

The last thing in the world that she looked like was a beer drinker.

"Surprised?" she said.

"No," I said, lying.

"You're not being truthful," she said, smiling at me. Those teeth were really something.

"OK, a little," I said. She had all the money. I'd play any game she wanted me to.

"People are always surprised when I say I want a beer. They naturally assume that I'm a champagne-type lady because of the way I look and dress, but looks can be deceiving."

When she'd said the word champagne, the chauffeur's neck twitched violently.

"Mr. Card?" she said.

"Oh," I said, looking from the chauffeur's neck back to her.

"Don't you think so?" she said. "Or are you a person who's taken in by looks?"

As I said, it was her money and I wanted some.

"To be honest with you, lady, I'm surprised that you're a beer drinker."

"Call me Miss Ann," she said.

"OK, Miss Ann, I'm surprised that you prefer beer to champagne."

The chauffeur's neck twitched violently again.

What in the hell was happening?

"Are you a champagne man?" she said, and as soon as she said the word champagne the chauffeur's neck twitched again. It was a twitch that looked powerful enough to break your thumb if you were touching his neck when the twitch went off. This guy's neck was something to be reckoned with.

"Mr. Card, did you hear me?" she said. "Are you a champagne man? Do you like champagne?"

The neck went off again like a gorilla rattling the bars of its cage.

"No, I like bourbon," I said. "Old Crow on the rocks."

The chauffeur's neck stopped twitching.

"How droll," she said. "We're going to have a wonderful time together."

"What are we going to do?" I said.

"Don't worry," she said. "There's plenty of time for that."

The chauffeur's neck remained quiet as we drove through San Francisco toward the Golden Gate Bridge. I could see that his neck had the potential for providing trouble in the future. I thought of what might happen if you crossed that neck. I didn't like that idea at all. I was going to keep on the good side of the neck. That neck and I were going to be close buddies if I had my way about it.

The neck didn't like the word champagne.

I would be very careful to avoid using that word in the future.

The neck liked the word bourbon, so that was a word that the neck was going to hear a lot of.

What in the hell was I getting myself into?

We drove down Lombard Street toward the Golden Gate Bridge and what I was going to get myself into.

Smith Smith Versus the Shadow Robots

Halfway across the Golden Gate Bridge, sitting beside a beautiful rich dame with a gigantic and very unstable neck driving the car, it came to me: the name for my serial about a private eye in Babylon. I would call it *Smith Smith Versus the Shadow Robots*. What a great title! I was almost beside myself with joy.

"What is it?" my client said who hadn't spoken in a couple of minutes as we drove along.

I started to say outloud the title of my serial. It was involuntary but I was able to stop it after the first word blurted itself out.

"Smith—" I said, stopping the rest of the words by sitting a mental elephant down on my tongue.

"Smith?" my client said.

The neck of the chauffeur looked as if it were about to twitch. I sure as hell didn't want that.

"I just remembered that a friend of mine's birthday was yesterday and I forgot all about it," I said. "I was going to give him a present. His name is Smith. A wonderful guy. A fisherman. He's got a boat down on the wharf. I grew up with his son. We went to Galileo High School together."

"Oh," my rich blonde client said with a slightly bored tone to her voice. She didn't want to hear about a fisherman named Smith. I wondered how she would have reacted if I had finished what I started out to say: *Smith Smith Versus the Shadow Robots.*

I would have found it very interesting to see how she would have handled that one. Thank God I only said the word Smith. I might have been out a client or even worse that neck might have gone into action.

The neck was relaxed now, just driving the car across the bridge.

A freighter was going out on the tide.

Its lights floated on the water.

"I want you to steal a dead body," my client said.

The Morning Paper

"What?" I said because a what was certainly needed at this time and nothing else but a what would be adequate for the situation.

"I want you to steal a body from the morgue."

She didn't say anything else.

She had very blue eyes. Even in the semidarkness of the car the blue was easy to see. Her eyes were staring at me. They waited for me to respond.

The neck waited, too.

"Sure," I said. "If the money's interesting enough I'll have Abraham Lincoln's body on your doorstep tomorrow with the morning paper."

That was exactly what she wanted to hear.

The neck wanted to hear it, too.

"How does a thousand dollars sound?" she said.

"For a thousand dollars," I said, "I'll bring you a whole cemetery."

Beer Tastes on a Champagne Budget

The lights of San Francisco looked beautiful shining across the bay from where we were sitting in a little bar in Sausalito.

My client was enjoying a beer.

She took a great deal of pleasure from drinking it. She didn't drink the way you'd expect her to. There was nothing lady-like the way she handled her beer. She drank beer like a longshoreman on payday.

She'd taken her fur coat off and underneath she was wearing a dress that showed off a knockout figure. This whole thing was just like a pulp detective story. I couldn't believe it.

The neck was out in the car, waiting for us, so I felt a little more relaxed around her. If I wanted to I could use the word champagne without fear of the unknown. The world sure is a strange place. No wonder I spend so much time dreaming of Babylon. It's safer.

"Where is the body you want stolen?" I said, watching this delicate-looking rich dame belt down a gulp of beer. Then belch. "You really enjoy your beer, don't you?" I said.

"I have beer tastes on a champagne budget," she said.

When she said champagne I involuntarily looked around for the neck. Thank God it was in the car.

"Now about this body you want," I said.

"Where do they keep bodies?" she said as if I were a little slow.

"A lot of places," I said. "But mostly in the ground. Do I need a shovel for this job?"

"No, silly," she said. "The body's in the morgue. Isn't that a logical place to keep one?"

"Yeah," I said. "It'll do."

She took another huge gulp of beer.

I motioned to the cocktail waitress to bring us some more beer. While I did this my client finished off the one that was in front of her. I think she'd just set the world record for a rich woman drinking a beer. I don't think Johnny Weissmuller could have gone through a beer any faster.

The waitress put another beer down in front of her.

I was still dabbling in an Old Crow on the rocks that I had ordered when we first came into the place. It would be my only drink. I wasn't much of a drinking person: a drink now and then, and one was my limit.

She went at the second beer with the same relish she had applied to the first beer. She was right when she said that she was a beer drinker.

"Do you think you can handle stealing a body from the morgue?" she said.

"Yeah, I can handle it," I said.

Then something popped up like a shooting gallery rabbit in my mind. Peg-leg had told me that she'd looked at the body of the dead prostitute for possible identification as a relative but said it wasn't the right person and she'd been very cold about the whole thing as if looking at dead bodies was a normal part of her day.

I thought about her crying when she left the morgue.

This was getting interesting.

Playing it casual, I said, "Who's the body you want me to steal from the morgue?"

"Who it is isn't important," she said. "That's my business. I just want you to get the body for me. It's the body of a young woman. She's upstairs in the autopsy room. There's a four-unit storage space for corpses built into the wall. She's on the top left side. She's got a Jane Doe tag on her big toe. Get her for me."

"OK," I said. "Where do you want the body after I get it?"

"I want you to take it to a cemetery," she said.

"That's simple enough," I said. "That's where bodies end up, anyway."

I ordered her another beer. She had already finished the second one. I had never seen a glass of beer look so empty, so fast before in my life. She practically breathed beer.

"Thank you," she said.

"When do you want the body?" I said.

"Tonight," she said. "Holy Rest Cemetery."

"That sounds soon enough," I said.

"May I ask what you're going to do with it?" I said.

"Come on, bright boy," she said. "What do you do with bodies in a cemetery?"

"OK," I said. "I get the picture. Do you want me to bring along a shovel?"

"No," she said. "You just bring the body to the cemetery and we'll take care of the rest. All we want from you is the body."

When she said we, I assumed what it took to make a we was the neck.

I ordered her another beer.

Earthquake in an Anvil Factory

"It's now seven-thirty," she said as we were sitting in the back seat of the limousine being driven back to San Francisco by the neck.

"I want the body at the cemetery at one A.M.," she said very succinctly, not showing in the slightest the effects of the six beers she'd put away in record time.

"OK," I said. "But if I'm late you can start without me."

The neck twitched in the front seat.

"Just kidding," I said.

"It's very important that the body be there at one A.M.," she said. She was sitting close to me and her breath hadn't the slightest scent of beer to it. Also, after finishing the six beers she got directly back into the car without going to the

126

toilet. I wondered where in the hell the beer had gone to.

"Don't worry," I said. "I'll have the body there on time."

"Good," she said.

I paused before I spoke again. I wanted the words that I was going to use to be the right ones. I didn't want any sloppy or inadequate words to come out of my mouth.

"I'll need half my fee up front," I said. "And also, I'll need three hundred dollars expense money. Some palms are going to have to be greased. I think you can appreciate the fact that stealing a body from the morgue is not your everyday run-of-the-mill thing. The city doesn't particularly like to lose bodies. People are prone to ask questions. It takes money to provide the answers."

"I understand," she said.

I looked over at her.

Where in the hell was that beer?

"Mr. Cleveland," she said to the neck driving the car. The neck reached into his coat pocket and took out a roll of bills and handed them back to me. The roll contained exactly eight hundred dollars in one hundred dollar bills. It was as if they had read my mind.

"Is that satisfactory?" she said.

I almost fainted when the money was handed to me. It had been a long time like light-years to the nearest star. I hadn't seen this much money since I'd gotten paid off for my automobile accident.

This was definitely the start of an upward trend in my life. I couldn't have been happier as I sat there driving across the Golden Gate Bridge and all I had to do to earn the money was to steal a corpse.

Then the neck spoke for the first time. A voice that

sounded like an earthquake in an anvil factory came from the front of the neck that didn't bother to turn its head toward me.

"Don't fuck up," the neck said. "We want that body."

The Private Detectives of San Francisco

I didn't take the neck seriously. Stealing that body would not be a difficult task at all. There would be nothing to it. It was as good as in the cemetery right now.

I felt wonderful as we went through the tollgate.

I was on top of the world.

Money again!

I'd be able to get some of my debts off my back and be able to have an office again and maybe even a part-time secretary. I could even afford an old car to get around in.

Things couldn't have looked better for me at that time. I was looking at the world through rose-colored glasses. It didn't even bother me that I couldn't figure out where six glasses of beer had disappeared to in my fancy client. They were there someplace. That's all I needed to know.

Something crossed my contented mind.

I couldn't resist asking about it.

"By the way," I said. "How did you hear about me? I mean, there are a lot more well-known private detectives in San Francisco. Why did you choose me?"

"You're the only one we could trust to steal a body for us," the rich blonde said. "The other detectives might have some scruples. You don't have any."

It was of course true.

I wasn't offended at all.

I didn't have anything to hide.

"Where did you hear about me?" I said.

"I have my sources," she said.

"Don't fuck up," the neck said.

Future Practice

I had them let me off at a fancy apartment building with a doorman a few blocks away from where I lived. I told them that's where I lived.

They pulled up in front of the place and let me out.

The doorman looked curiously at me.

"Thanks for taking me home," I said.

The neck turned toward me as I got out of the car and it spoke. "Why do you want to get out here?" it said. "You don't live here. You live in a rat-trap a couple of blocks away. But maybe you need the exercise. We don't care where you live. We just want that body at the south gate of Holy Rest Cemetery at one A.M. Sharp."

I stood there not being able to think of anything to say.

Who were these people? How did they know so much about me? I didn't think I was that popular.

"I'm practicing," I said, finally. "Someday I'll live here."

The neck started to speak again, "Don't—"

"I know," I said. "Fuck up."

"See you later, Mr. Card," the fancy blonde said to me with six glasses of beer hidden somewhere in her beautiful body.

The car drove slowly away.

I watched it until it turned a corner and was gone.

The doorman started sweeping the sidewalk. He was sweeping very close to me. I moved on.

C. Card,
Private Investigator

I still hadn't called my mother.

She was back from the cemetery by now.

I'd better get that done with. Also, I'd be able to tell her that I could repay some of the money that I had borrowed from her. Of course I wouldn't tell her the size of my fee because she'd want more money than I wanted to repay her.

I was very much interested now in getting an office, a secretary and a car. My mother could wait. She was used to it. She wouldn't do anything but put the money in the bank, and that's the last place in this world where I wanted my money.

I needed an office that had

C. Card
Private Investigator

in gold on the door, and I needed a gorgeous secretary taking dictation.

Dear Mr. Cupertino,

Thank you very much for the five-hundred-dollar bonus for finding your daughter. It's a pleasure to do business with a gentleman. If you ever lose her again, you know where to find me, and the next time it's on the house.

Yours sincerely,
C. Card

And I needed a car so I could get around town without wearing holes in my shoes. There's something about a private detective walking or taking the bus that lacks class.

It makes clients uncomfortable to meet a private detective who has a bus transfer sticking out of his shirt pocket.

But right now I'd better call my mother.

I walked a couple of blocks to a phone booth.

I dropped a nickel in and then put the receiver up to my ear. There was no dial tone. I pressed the coin return but my nickel stayed inside the telephone. I clicked the telephone hook. Silence continued inside the receiver, and it was not golden. It was my fucking nickel.

God-damn it!

I was out a nickel.

Big business had fucked me over again.

I hit the telephone a couple of times with my fist to make

the point that some people won't take being robbed without putting up a fight.

I left the phone booth and walked half a block.

I turned around and looked angrily back at the telephone.

An old man was standing inside the booth. He had the receiver in his hand and he was talking to somebody on the telephone.

You just can't win.

I wondered if the old man was using his nickel or perhaps in some totally unjust way he had managed to make his call as the result of my nickel.

The only revenge I got out of the situation was the thought that if he was making that call with my nickel, I hoped that he was calling his doctor to get some relief from a hideous attack of hemorrhoids.

That was the only way that I was going to come out on top of this bad deal.

I turned around and walked to the bus stop on Clay Street. I was going to take the bus down to the morgue. I could have gotten a cab but I decided to take the bus as a sort of farewell bus trip because I was never going to have to ride a bus again.

This was the last time.

A young woman was waiting for the bus.

She was kind of good looking, so I decided to try out my new affluence by giving her a big smile and saying good evening.

She didn't return the smile and she didn't say good evening.

She nervously turned her back on me.

Suddenly the bus loomed up a block away.

135

A minute later I was sitting on the bus heading back down to the morgue. I got on the bus first and when I sat down in a front seat, the young woman went to the back of the bus.

I've just never been a lady's man but that was all going to change as soon as I stole that body and got the rest of my fee and became the most famous private detective in San Francisco, make that California, no, let's make it America. Why settle for less than the whole God-damn country?

I already had a foolproof plan to steal the body.

Nothing could go wrong.

It was perfect.

So I settled back in my seat and started dreaming of Babylon. My mind slipped effortlessly back into the past. I was no longer on the bus. I was in Babylon.

Chapter 1 /
Smith Smith Versus
the Shadow Robots

Deep in the hidden recesses of his cellar laboratory hidden under the clinic that he used to lure unsuspecting sick people into only to change them into shadow robots, Dr. Abdul Forsythe was removing a person who had been changed into a shadow from his diabolical transformation chamber.

"This is a good one," he said, examining the texture of the shadow.

"You're a genius," his henchman Rotha said, standing beside the doctor, looking at the shadow. After admiring his handiwork, Dr. Abdul Forsythe gave the shadow to Rotha who took it over and put it on top of a six-foot pile of shadows. There were a thousand shadows in the pile. There were a dozen or so piles in the laboratory.

Dr. Forsythe had enough shadows to create an artificial night large enough to take over a small town. He only lacked one thing to put his plot into action. That one ingredient was the mercury crystals that had just been invented by Dr. Francis, a humanitarian doctor who had devoted his life to good works in Babylon. He lived near the Ishtar Gate with his beautiful daughter Cynthia who had a half-sister named Nana-dirat.

Dr. Francis had invented the mercury crystals to power a rocket ship that he was constructing to fly to the moon with.

After Rotha had put the shadow of an unfortunate sandal maker, who'd come to the clinic to have a sore looked at but had stayed to end up as a shadow and part of a diabolical plan, on the pile, he returned to the side of his evil master.

"Now what, boss?" Rotha said.

"The mercury crystals," Dr. Abdul Forsythe said. "Then we're in business." They both laughed fiendishly. You could tell by the way they laughed that the business they were involved in did not have retirement benefits. There was no pension for what they were doing.

Quickdraw Artist

Suddenly I realized where I was at and like a quickdraw artist in a cowboy movie my hand flew up and pulled the cord to stop the bus. I got it just in time.

Another few seconds and I would have missed my stop. Dreaming of Babylon is a tricky business.

One miscalculation and you're blocks beyond your stop.

Fortunately, this was my last bus trip and I wouldn't have to worry about missing my stop any more. Thank God. Once I went all the way to the end of the line dreaming of Babylon and I didn't have enough money to get back and the driver wouldn't let me ride for free, even after I had explained to him that I didn't have any money and told a lie to him, that I had fallen asleep.

"I hear stories like this all the time," he said, with a remarkable lack of concern for my plight. "You can't ride my bus with stories for a fare. I want a nickel. If you don't have a nickel, get off my bus. I don't make the rules. It costs a nickel to ride. I'm just a working stiff, so get off my bus."

I didn't like the way the son-of-a-bitch kept saying "my bus" as if he owned the God-damn thing.

"Do you own this bus?" I said.

"What do you mean?" he said.

"I mean, do you own this bus? You keep saying 'my bus' so I thought maybe you owned the fucking bus and you take it home with you and sleep with it. Maybe you're even married to it. This bus is your wife."

I didn't get to say anything else because the bus driver knocked me unconscious with one blow right there from his seat. It was lights out. I came to about ten minutes later, sitting on the sidewalk, leaning up against the front of a drugstore.

To have the perfect ending for a bus trip was what woke me up. It was a dog peeing on me. Maybe he thought that I looked like a fire hydrant. Anyway, those days were over. I had eight hundred bucks in my pocket and this had been my last bus trip.

When I got off the bus, I turned around and yelled "Fuck you!" at the driver. He looked bewildered. It served him right. No more dogs were going to pee on me.

Ghouls

As I walked into the morgue two guys were walking out carrying a large bag between them. You couldn't tell what was in the bag but it was heavy. They seemed to be in quite a hurry. There was a car double-parked in front of the morgue and the trunk was open. They put the bag in the trunk, closed it and drove off. They were in such a hurry that the rear tires screeched when they drove away.

I wondered briefly what was in the bag. It was kind of late to be taking things out of the morgue but obviously they had a reason because that's what they had just done. I walked back into the morgue, looking for Peg-leg but I couldn't find him. He wasn't in the autopsy room or downstairs in "cold storage" with his beloved stiffs. I walked back out into the front hall and there was Peg-leg coming in the door. He had a paper bag in his hand. He pegged down the hall toward me.

"Well," he said. "If it isn't a sight for poor eyes. What are you doing back here? Looking for a partner who's as bad a dancer as you are? Well, we got 'em. Dead people dance almost as badly as you do, 'Eye.' "

That was a joke that Peg-leg liked to repeat as often as he could. We'd once gone dancing together on a double-date with a couple of stenographers. I've always been a terrible dancer. He thought it was really funny watching me try to dance with a dumb redhead.

Peg-leg of course is a great dancer. It always amazes people. Often a whole dance hall will come to a complete stop with everybody standing there watching Peg-leg dance. They can't believe it. When I dance nobody cares.

People have even suggested seriously that Peg-leg open up a dance studio like Arthur Murray.

I'd like to see that.

"What have you got in the bag?" I said, changing the subject away from my dancing.

"A sandwich and you can't have any. It's my dinner. What are you doing here, anyway, 'Eye?' Returning my gun and paying back the fifty you owe me? I sure hope so, but I don't think my heart could take it."

"No," I said. "I've got a business proposition for you."

"You're too broke to have a business proposition," Peg-leg said. "So what do you really want?"

"I'm not kidding," I said. "I've got a bona fide proposition and some money to back it up."

"Money?" he said. "You?"

"Yeah, my bad-luck streak is over. I'm on my way to the top. Nothing can stop me."

"I know you're not a drinking man, 'Eye,' so you've got to be sober. Jesus. First, Pearl Harbor and now you've got a business proposition. What next? Let's go back to my office and talk about this, but you'd better not be pulling my leg because if you do you're going to get some splinters in your hand."

Peg-leg's "office" was a desk in the autopsy room.

I walked behind Peg-leg who was agilely moving along on his wooden stem.

"Hey," I said, suddenly remembering the two men and the bag they were carrying. "Did you have something picked up here a few minutes ago?"

"What do you mean?" Peg-leg said.

"Two men walked out of here with a large bag full of something."

"No," Peg-leg said. "Nobody was supposed to pick up anything here. It's too late for pickups. I think the City and County of San Francisco just got robbed. I wonder what they took. What in the hell can you steal from a morgue? We've only got one thing here. I mean, this isn't a grocery store." When he said that, he stopped talking and looked very seriously at me. Then he scratched his chin and sighed.

"As I said," he said. "We've only got one thing here and I think we're probably one less now."

"Are you thinking what I'm starting to think?" I said, starting to think it.

"Yup," he said. "Ghouls."

Cold Heartless Cash

We walked back to Peg-leg's "office"—the autopsy room.

When we got there Peg-leg stood for a few seconds in front of a small icebox for dead people that was built into one wall. It was a mini-refrigerator that had enough space for four corpses. The rest of the stiffs were kept downstairs in a big cold storage room. The ones they kept upstairs were special. I don't know why. I never asked. I didn't care.

I thought that Peg-leg was going to check the icebox to see if anybody was missing from there but instead he walked over to his desk and sat down and took his sandwich out of the paper bag. He motioned toward the coffee pot that was on a hot plate on the desk beside him. "Get yourself a cup," he said, then motioning toward an autopsy sink that had some cups beside it. "Pour me some while you're at it. I'm going to eat my sandwich while it's still hot."

"What about the missing body?" I said, going over to the autopsy sink and getting the cups.

"It's still going to be gone by the time my sandwich cools off. I didn't get a hot sandwich to eat it cold. Do you know what I mean?"

"Yeah," I said. "I understand. I just wondered who would steal a body from the morgue."

"I told you," Peg-leg said, taking a bite out of a bacon, lettuce and tomato sandwich, the old BLT. His words became entangled with the sandwich but I could still make them out. "Ghouls," he said. "But why in the hell couldn't they get a body from the cemetery? Why did they want one of mine?"

"Maybe they wanted a fresh one instead of a stale one," I said.

"That sounds logical," Peg-leg said. "Sort of. I guess."

I poured two cups of Peg-leg's coffee and took a sip of mine. I grimaced as the fluid hit my taste buds. His coffee had the same effect as being whacked in the mouth with a baseball bat.

"You could raise the dead with this coffee," I said.

"Don't think I haven't thought about it," Peg-leg said. "Especially that little whore they brought in this morning."

"You mean the one you were getting ready to fuck when I came by earlier?" I said.

"I wasn't going to fuck her," Peg-leg said. "I don't know where you get ideas like that. Just say I'm a fan of the human body. I like its contours and lines."

"That's a different way of putting it," I said. "From where I was standing you looked about five seconds away from humping her."

"Hey, what are you doing down here again?" Peg-leg said, changing the subject.

"I told you," I said. "I've got a business proposition for you. You can make some money."

"What do you mean *make* some money?" Peg-leg said. "You already *owe* me some money. When are you going to pay up? That's the cash I'm interested in."

"Right now," I said and reached into my pocket. I knew that I was going to have to repay him the money I owed him before I could get on with my business transaction.

"Here's a hundred," I said, liking this part a lot. "Now you owe me some money, Keeper of Dead People."

Peg-leg couldn't believe the hundred dollar bill in his clammy hand. He stared at it as if it were a miracle. He was suddenly a very happy Peg-leg.

"It must be real. I know it's not a mirage because I can feel it in my hand. What's the business proposition?" Peg-leg said. "I want more of this stuff. I know exactly where to spend it."

"There's two hundred dollars more where that came from," I said.

"Hurray!" Peg-leg said. "What do I have to do?"

"You have a car, don't you?" I said.

"Yeah, an old Plymouth," Peg-leg said. "You know the car. Why?"

"I want to borrow it," I said.

"Consider it yours, old pal," Peg-leg said. "Where's

the two hundred? This is the easiest money I've ever made."

"That's not all I want," I said. "There's something else. I want to put it in the trunk."

"I'll help," Peg-leg said. "Where are the C notes?"

"Don't you want to know what I want you to help me put in the trunk?" I said.

"For two hundred dollars I don't care what you're going to put in the trunk," Peg-leg said. "I'll help. I'm your man. Where's it at?" He was staring happily at the hundred dollar bill in his hand.

"Here," I said.

"What?" Peg-leg said, looking up.

"You've got what I want to put in the trunk right here," I said.

Peg-leg looked puzzled. He was mulling it over in his mind. It didn't take him long. I could see that he was mentally approaching what I wanted. Then he was there.

"What in the hell is going on? You're not thinking what I think you're thinking?" Peg-leg said. "No, not two of them in the same night. Tell me I'm wrong."

"You're right," I said. "It's a strange world. I've been hired to steal a stiff and you've got the body the people want right here."

"What do they want a dead body for?" Peg-leg said.

"Lonely, I guess. I don't know," I said. "It's their business and I don't care just as long as I see some long green looking up at me from my palm. Are you still interested in the two hundred?"

"Sure," Peg-leg said. "I don't care. I'm already out one

corpse today and I didn't get a cent for it or even a thank you. It's just as easy to explain the absence of two bodies as it is one. I'm your man. Let me see the two hundred and take your pick."

I gave him the two hundred.

He was ecstatic.

"Take your pick," Peg-leg said, making a grandiose circle in the air with the hand that contained the money. "Take your pick. You can have anyone you want."

"I'm sorry but I'm going to have to break up your romance," I said. "I hope I don't break your heart but somebody will come along to replace her. Women are dying all the time."

"Oh, no," Peg-leg said. "Not her. She's my favorite."

"I'm sorry, pal," I said.

He shook his head.

"I'll get her for you," Peg-leg said.

"I'm surprised at you," I said. "Selling your sweetie for cold heartless cash. How can you do it?"

"Easy," Peg-leg said. "She's heartless, too. We did an autopsy on her while you were gone."

Time Heals
All Wounds

Peg-leg finished eating his BLT.

"Let's get your body for you," he said. "I hate to see her go. She's the prettiest corpse I've had here in years."

"You'll get over it," I said. "Time heals all wounds."

"No," Peg-leg said. "Two hundred bucks does."

"Where's she at?" I said, pretending that I didn't already know. Don't ask me why.

Peg-leg pointed over at the four-corpse refrigerator in the autopsy room. "Top left," he said.

I walked over to the refrigerator, opened the top left door and started to pull the tray out.

"No, it's the top right," Peg-leg said. "I forgot. I moved her. She's in the top right."

"I know. There's nobody in here," I said. I was going to tell Peg-leg but he told me first.

"What?" Peg-leg said and walked over to the refrigerator. "There should be a corpse in there. I put one in there a few hours ago. What in the hell is going on?" He looked inside as if the corpse were hiding in there and he was going to find it. "God-damn it! There was a divorcée in here when I went out to get my sandwich and now she's gone. She killed herself this afternoon. Climbed into an oven with the gas on. Where did she go? I mean, she was dead."

"That's your problem," I said. "I just paid you two hundred dollars for the body of a dead whore, and I want her. She's over here on the left, huh? Are you sure?"

"Yeah," Peg-leg said, shaking his head over the absence of the divorcée's corpse. "Over here." He pulled out the tray, lifted up the sheet and there she was. "See, two hundred dollars' worth. But where did that other body go? It was here a couple of hours ago. Now it's gone. What in the hell is going on in this place?"

Suddenly a thought came to my mind.

Thank God it wasn't about Babylon.

"Wait a minute," I said. "I'll bet you anything she was the body the two guys stole from here a little while ago."

"I think you're right, 'Eye,' " Peg-leg said. "You are right. That's the only thing that could have happened. They stole the divorcée. Why would anyone want her body? She was real ugly. A wino. I don't know why anyone would want her. She was a total mess. I think she did herself and the world a favor by getting in the oven."

Interesting, I thought. There seemed to be more to this than met the eye. I wondered if perhaps those two guys had gotten the wrong body, and the body they had intended to steal was the one I was looking at.

This was starting to get complicated.

Maybe this wasn't going to be as easy as it had looked in the beginning. Suddenly I was very glad that I had a gun in my pocket with some bullets in it. Who knows? That gun might come in handy.

Yeah, the night had the possibility of being a long one and I'd better keep on my toes. The first thing I had to do was to get the body I was being paid to steal out of the morgue. When those guys found out that they had the wrong body they might come back looking for the right one and they might not be nice about it.

The
Jack Benny Show

"Let's get this thing out of here," I said.

"Listen, 'Eye,'" Peg-leg said. "Don't talk like that about her. She doesn't like being dead any more than you would. OK?"

I'd gotten Peg-leg's dandruff up.

"I'm sorry," I said, though I wasn't sorry at all. I just wanted to get on with it.

"I'll find something to put her into," Peg-leg said, pacified.

"Where's your car?" I said.

"Parked across the street," Peg-leg said. "I always park it across the street."

He pegged over and opened up a closet door. There was a pile of corpse-dirty laundry beside a full laundry bag.

"God-damn it! The bastards stole my laundry bag," Peg-leg said, opening up the other laundry bag and dumping its contents on top of the other pile. "This makes two of them they stole," he said. "Anyway, that's what I'm going to tell the police after you give me a punch on the jaw, so I can have a good alibi for this caper. I'll tell them that two body snatchers raided the icebox. I put up a good fight but they knocked me out. Maybe I'll even get a medal and the mayor will shake my cold, cold hand."

We put the young prostitute's body in the laundry bag. Peg-leg did a good job of folding her up.

"You're pretty good at this kind of business," I said.

"I should be," Peg-leg said. "I got a gold watch last year for my ten thousandth corpse." He gave her a little pat on the head before pulling the strings that closed the top of the laundry bag over her head.

"Good-bye, baby," Peg-leg said. "I'll miss you."

"Don't worry," I said. "You'll catch up with her later on."

"Funny man," Peg-leg said. "You should be on the *Jack Benny Show*."

A Strange Cup of Sugar from Oakland

Peg-leg helped me carry her out to his car.

I was smiling as we toted her along.

Peg-leg looked curiously at me. "Let me in on it," he said.

"I was just thinking," I said. "There sure are a lot of bodies going out of this place in laundry bags. If it keeps up at this rate, you'll be out of bodies by the end of the week, and to be a respectable big-city morgue, you'll have to borrow some from Oakland."

"I wish I hadn't asked," Peg-leg said.

We were now halfway across the street carrying the body between us.

Peg-leg opened up the trunk of his car and we put the body in. He closed the lid and handed me the keys.

"Hey, what about my gun?" Peg-leg said. "When are you going to return it? With body thieves running all over the God-damn place, present company included, I need my cannon. I don't know what in the hell is going to happen in there next." He motioned with his head toward the morgue that was running out of bodies at a very fast clip.

"The gun's part of the two hundred," I said. "I'll return it tomorrow with your car."

"You strike a hard bargain," Peg-leg said.

"Do you want your body back?" I said.

"Nope."

"You always were a fickle one with the ladies," I said. "Are you sure you don't want her back?"

"She's yours," Peg-leg said. "I'll take the two hundred and buy a piece of ass from a live one." He started back across the street, then he stopped in his tracks, one of which was wooden. "Hey," he said. "You forgot to hit me on the jaw. My alibi. Remember?"

"Sure," I said. "Bring your jaw back here."

I hit him on the jaw.

His head snapped back four inches.

"Does that do it?" I said.

Peg-leg was rubbing his jaw.

"Yeah, that does it. Thanks, 'Eye.' "

"Don't mention it."

He pegged back into the morgue.

Warner Brothers

I got into the front seat of the car and put the key into the ignition. All I had to do now was drive around for a few hours and kill some time until 1 A.M. and body-delivery time at Holy Rest Cemetery.

Before I could get the car started, another car pulled up opposite me and two guys got out. They looked very angry. They seemed familiar. Then I recognized them. They were the same guys who had stolen the body of the divorcée a little while ago.

They were really pissed off.

There was a third guy in the driver's seat.

When they got out of the car, he drove off.

The guys walked very business-like, as if they were characters in a Warner Brothers' gangster movie, into the morgue. They weren't fooling around.

One of the guys was very large with a square build.

He looked like a ham with legs.

Peg-leg was really going to earn his two hundred and fifty dollars.

I drove off.

The Babylon-Orion Express

A morgue scene would be a very good one to include in Smith Smith Versus the Shadow Robots, I thought as I drove down Columbus Avenue with the girl's body safely in the trunk.

I envisioned Nana-dirat and I going into the city morgue of Babylon to identify a body. It was night and foggy in Babylon as we walked down the street to the morgue. We were a block away.

"You don't have to do this," I said. "It might be a little grizzly. The guy was hit by a train. There's very little left to identify. You might want to wait outside for me."

"No," she said. "I want to go with you. I don't like to have you out of my sight if I can help it. You know how stuck on you I am. You're my guy, you big lug. I don't care if that guy was hit by three Babylon-Orion Expresses."

Nana-dirat really had a crush on me.

"OK," I said. "But remember I warned you."

"Make that six Babylon-Orion Expresses," Nana-dirat said.

What a gal!

A private eye couldn't have a better secretary in Babylon.

Partners in Mayhem

Ah, shit . . . good-bye, Babylon.

I turned the car around at Union Street and drove back to the morgue. Try as I could, I just couldn't leave old Peg-leg to provide amusement for those goons.

Peg-leg's parking place was available right across the street from the morgue, so I pulled in there. I looked around for the goons' car but it was nowhere in sight. I slipped out of the car like the shadow of a banana peeling and walked quickly but almost anonymously into the morgue.

I had my hand in my coat pocket, fingering the loaded pistol. I was ready for business and I wanted some answers to why in the hell these guys were stealing bodies from the morgue. I was going to find out what was happening.

That's what private detectives are supposed to do and if I had to get a little rough it was totally acceptable in the tradition.

I was halfway down the hall toward the autopsy room when I heard a crash and a moan. Those bastards were already working poor Peg-leg over.

They would pay for it.

I stood outside the closed door with the gun in my hand, ready to spring inside and give those guys quite a surprise. I heard another moan and then another crash. There was silence for a few seconds and then a horrible scream—

AAAHHHHHHHHHHHHHHHHHHH!

A sound from hell was the cue to my grand entrance.

I sprung into the autopsy room and there was quite a sight waiting for me like some kind of strange greeting card. First of all, Peg-leg was sitting at his desk with a cup of coffee in his hand. He was as relaxed and cool as a cucumber. He wasn't even startled as I flew into the room.

"Welcome to the party," he said like a host, motioning toward the activities that were going on in the room. There was another blood-curdling scream, "AAAHHHHHHHHH-HHHHH! Don't put me back in here! For God's sake! AAAHHHHHHHHHHHH! AAAHHHHHHHHHHHHHHH!"

In the corner of the autopsy room was the body of one of the hoods. He was very unconscious. He looked as if he were going to hibernate for the winter.

Sergeant Rink was standing beside the open door of one of the death icebox trays. The second hood was lying hand-cuffed on the tray. He was the one who was doing all the screaming. He had been pushed about ninety percent of the way into the refrigerator for dead people and he didn't care for that at all. All you could see of him was his face that was totally terrified to the point of almost going mad.

"AAAHHHHHHHHHHHHHHHH!" he screamed.

"One more time," Sergeant Rink said. "What in the fuck are you up to going around stealing dead bodies and trying to beat up morgue attendants who happen to be my friends?"

"I'll tell you anything just don't put me in here with the dead people," the hood said. He had a good point. It was not a pleasant place to be. I certainly would not have wanted to be in his shoes which were now growing cold.

Sergeant Rink pulled him out a ways, so that you could see his belt buckle.

"Is that better?" he said to the hood.

"Yes, thank you," the goon responded with a sudden, joyous look of relief on his face.

"OK, insect, spill it."

Sergeant Rink had a reputation of being a very tough cop and it was a reputation that he lived up to 100%. I really had to admire him. Too bad Babylon had gotten the best of me when I was going to the police academy with him. We might have turned out to be partners together. I liked that idea a lot.

Oh, well, I also liked Babylon a lot, too. Even though things had been a bit hard, I had no regrets about dreaming of Babylon all the time.

Sergeant Rink had been so involved with interrogating the goon that he hadn't responded to me running into the autopsy room with a gun in my hand or he had recognized that it was me and I didn't require that much immediate attention.

But now he was looking at me.

He had diverted his attention from the gorilla who had just become a canary.

"I was hired—" the goon started to say.

"Shut up, roach," Sergeant Rink said, diverting his attention to me. The "roach" shut up. He didn't want to spend the night in the freezer with what few bodies were left in the morgue that somehow had avoided being stolen that night.

"Hi, Card," Rink said. "Why the pistola? and what in the hell are you doing here, anyway?"

"I came to visit Peg-leg and I heard some loud activity going on in here," I said. "I knew that something had to be up because they keep dead people in here and they aren't famous for causing a commotion, so I came in prepared for action. What's up?" I said, praying to God that Peg-leg hadn't spilled the beans on me being one of the people who had taken a fresh body from the place and happily put it in the trunk of a car.

"Caught some ghouls here," Sergeant Rink said. "They stole two bodies from Peg-leg and then they came back and tried to work him over while they stole some more. Sons-of-bitches. I've been giving them a little lesson in crime doesn't pay."

He casually pushed the hood back into the refrigerator until only his eyes were staring out at us.

"AAAHHHHHHHHHHHHHHH!" the hood responded to being pushed back into the refrigerator.

"See, crime doesn't pay," Rink said to the hood as he pushed the tray all the way in and then closed the door. We could hear the muffled screams of the man coming from the refrigerator.

"aaahhhhhhhhhhhh . . . aaahhhhhhhhh . . . aaahhhhhhhhhhh . . ."

Sergeant Rink walked over and poured himself a cup of morgue coffee. "I'll leave him in there for a little while. Let him cool his heels. He won't be stealing any more bodies when I'm through with that bastard."

Rink took a sip of coffee.

He didn't even grimace.

He was one hell-of-a tough cop.

Muffled screams kept coming from the freezer.

"aaahhhhhhhhhhhhhhhh . . ."

. . . on and on.

It didn't seem to bother Peg-leg or Rink, so I didn't let it bother me.

Today
Is My Lucky Day

I got a cup and joined Peg-leg and Sergeant Rink in some coffee while the goon continued screaming, tucked away on his tray in the city refrigerator.

"I told Sergeant Rink just before you jumped in here, 'Eye,' which I appreciate a lot, shit, if the sergeant hadn't come along you'd be my hero, that these guys stole two bodies from me today," Peg-leg said. "I don't know what in the hell they wanted two bodies for. They were just getting ready to work me over again when the sergeant came by. What a break. Today is my lucky day."

Peg-leg was looking directly into my eyes when he said, "Lucky day." I appreciated it. Of course two hundred and fifty bucks in your pocket isn't exactly a horse laugh.

"I'll find out why these guys stole those bodies," Sergeant Rink said. "I'll let our friend stay in the cooler until we finish our coffee. He'll be ready to talk by then and I don't think he'll want to steal any more bodies. He'll be reformed, the fucking desecrater."

His screams continued to work their way out of the cooler. They never stopped. The guy sounded as if he were going insane in there.

"You have no idea why these guys wanted to steal those bodies, huh?" Sergeant Rink said to Peg-leg.

"None," Peg-leg said. "I think they're just a pair of fucking ghouls. Bela Lugosi would be proud to know these jerks."

"What bodies did they take?" Rink said.

"Two women," Peg-leg said. "A suicide divorcée, no loss, and the body of that murdered whore you brought in earlier."

"Her, huh?" the sergeant said. "She was a good-looking woman. Too bad. So those creeps stole her body. This is getting a little more interesting."

The ghoul hood continued screaming from the icebox.

"I think he's almost ready," Rink said. "I don't think I'm going to have any trouble getting the truth out of him."

The other hood continued to hibernate on the floor in the corner. He sure was unconscious. When Rink puts them out, they stay out.

"*aaahhhhhhhhh . . . aaahhhhhhhhh . . . aaahhhhhhhh*"
. . . continued to come from the refrigerator.

Sergeant Rink took another sip of coffee.

166

The Sahara Desert

Just about that time the third hood came strolling into the autopsy room, looking for his amigos in body theft. He was greeted by the sight of one of his buddies lying in a very unconscious heap in the corner and he could hear the muffled screams of his other partner coming from the icebox.

The hood turned white as a sheet.

"Wrong room," he said. The words were very dry when they came out of his mouth. He sounded like the Sahara Desert talking.

"Excuse me," he said, turning around with great difficulty and heading unevenly toward the sanctuary of the door which must have seemed like a million miles away to him.

167

He had just been turned from a living, breathing hood to a cardboard cutout of a hood.

"Wait a minute, citizen," Sergeant Rink said, and then took a casual sip of his coffee. "Where in the fuck do you think you're going?"

The hood stopped dead in his tracks which was very appropriate for the place that he was at.

"I've got the wrong address," he said, Sahara-ily.

Sergeant Rink shook his head very slowly.

"Do you mean this is the right address?" the hood said, not knowing what he was saying, his brain hypnotized by fear.

Sergeant Rink nodded his head, yes, this was the right place.

"Sit down, fuckball," the sergeant said, motioning toward a chair on the far side of the room right beside the body of the sleeping bear-like hood.

"Fuckball" started to say something but Sergeant Rink shook his head, no. The hood let out a huge sigh that could have filled a clipper sail. He started walking very unsure of himself as if on a stormy deck toward the chair.

The screams continued coming from the refrigerator.

"aaahhhhhhhhhhhh . . . aaahhhhhhhh . . . aaahhhhhhhhh"

"Wait a minute," Rink said to the hood. "Do you have a heater?"

The hood stopped in his tracks and stood there as if he were frozen. He was staring at the icebox where the screams were coming from. He looked as if he were in a dream. He slowly nodded his head that he had a gun.

"That's not a nice boy," Sergeant Rink said fatherly, but

he sounded like a father whose business was a pitchfork factory in hell. "I bet you don't have a permit either."

The gunsel shook his head that he didn't have a permit. Then he spoke with great difficulty. "Why's he in there?" he said.

"Do you want to join him?"

"NO!" the crook yelled.

He was very emphatic about not wanting to get into the refrigerator with his comrade.

"Then be a good boy and I won't put you in with the dead people."

The hood nodded his head very emphatically that he wanted to be a good boy.

"Take the gun slowly out of your pocket and don't point it at anybody. Guns sometimes go off accidentally and we wouldn't want that to happen because somebody might get hurt and then somebody would spend their school vacation in the refrigerator with the dead people."

The crook took a .45 so slowly out of his pocket that he reminded me of trying to get very cold maple syrup out of a bottle.

The sergeant just sat there with the cup of coffee in his hand. He was a very cool customer and I could have been his partner if Babylon hadn't gotten the best of me.

"Bring the gun over here," the sergeant said.

The crook brought the gun over to the sergeant.

He was carrying the .45 as if he were a girl scout with a box of cookies in his hand.

"Hand me the gun."

He handed the gun to the sergeant.

"Now go put your ass down on that chair and I don't want

to hear anything out of you," Rink said. "I want you to become a statue. Do you understand?"

"Yes."

It was a yes that sounded as if it really wanted to go and sit down and become a living statue.

The hood took the yes over to the chair beside his sleeping chum and sat down. He did just what the sergeant said and became a statue of failed criminality. He had pointed himself marbly in the direction of the icebox. He sat there staring at it and listening to the screams coming from it.

"aaahhhh ! ! ! aaahhhhh ! ! ! aaahhhhh ! ! ! aaahhhh!!!"

. . . coming now in short gasps.

"Just like the Shadow says," Sergeant Rink said. " 'Crime doesn't pay.' "

"aaahhhh ! ! ! aaahhhh ! ! ! ahhhh ! ! ! aaahhhh ! ! !"

"I think this fucker is ready to sing now," Rink said. "I'm going to get to the bottom of this. Morgues shouldn't be this exciting. The city of San Francisco can't afford to have its corpses pickpocketed. It gives the town a bad reputation among dead people."

"aaahhhh ! ! ! aaahhhh ! ! ! aaahhhh ! ! ! aaahhhh !!!"

. . . continuing to come from the refrigerator.

"Any operas you guys want to hear?" the sergeant said.

"La Traviata," I said.

"Madam Butterfly," Peg-leg said.

"Coming up," Rink said.

The Edgar Allan Poe Hotfoot

There are no words to describe the expression on the hood's face when Sergeant Rink pulled him out of the refrigerator. He opened it up just a crack at first. You could only see the guy's eyes. They looked as if Edgar Allan Poe had given them both hotfoots.

He was screaming as the tray was slowly pulled out.

"AAAHHHHHHH! AAAHHHHHHH! AAAHHH-HHH! AAAHHHHHHHHH!"

. . . with those eyes looking wildly at us.

"Shut up," Rink said.

"AAAH—" The hood shut totally up as if an invisible Mount Everest had been dropped on his mouth.

The expression in his eyes changed from Poe-esque terror

171

to an unbelievable dimension of silent pleading. He looked as if he were asking the Pope for a miracle.

"Would you like to come out a little further into the world of the living?" Rink said.

The hood nodded his head and tears started flowing from his eyes.

The sergeant pulled the tray out until his entire face was visible. He pulled it out very slowly. Then he stopped and stood there, staring down at the destroyed hood. A benevolent smile crept its way onto Rink's features. He patted the terrified hood on the cheek affectionately with his hand.

Mother Rink.

"Ready to sing?"

The hood nodded his head.

"I want it all, right from the top or back in you go and I might not take you out the next time. Also, I'm not above embalming a cheap rat like you alive. Get the picture?"

Mother Rink.

The hood nodded his head again.

"OK, tell me all about it."

"I don't know where she put all the beer," the hood started talking hysterically. "She had ten beers and she didn't go to the toilet. She just kept drinking beer and not going to the toilet. She was so skinny. There was no place for the beer to go inside her body but she just kept packing it away. She had at least ten beers. There was no room for the beer!" he screamed. "No room!"

"Who was that?" the sergeant said.

"The woman who hired us to steal the body. She was a beer drinker. God, I never saw anything like it. The beer just kept disappearing."

"Who was she?" Rink said.

"She didn't tell us. She just wanted the body. No questions asked. Good money. We didn't know this was going to happen. She was a rich dame. My father told me never to get involved with rich dames. Look at me. I'm in a cooler full of dead people. I can smell them. They're dead. Why in the hell didn't I listen to him?"

"You should have listened to your father," Rink said.

Just then the hood lying in the corner started coming to. The sergeant looked over at the statue of a hood sitting in a chair above him.

"Your friend's coming to," he said to the hood. "Kick him in the head for me. He needs some more rest."

The hood in the chair, without standing up because he hadn't been told to stand up, kicked the other hood in the head. He went back to sleep.

"Thank you," Rink said and then went back to grilling the hood handcuffed on the tray. "Do you have any idea why she wanted the body?"

"No, she just drank beer all the time. The money was good. I didn't know this was going to happen. We were just going to steal a body."

"Was she alone?" Rink said.

"No, she had a bodyguard chauffeur-type with a big neck like a fire hydrant. We came here and got a body but it was the wrong one, so we came back for the right one but it wasn't here. We weren't really going to hurt your one-legged pal. We were just going to rough him up a little bit, so we could get the right body."

"What body were you going for?" Rink said.

"The whore who got knocked off today."

"Did you kill her?"

"No! No, oh, God, no!" the hood said. He didn't like that question at all.

"Don't use the word God around here, you little prick, or I'll stick you back in the freezer."

The sergeant was an Irish Catholic who went to Mass every Sunday.

"I'm sorry! I'm sorry," the hood said. "Don't put me back in there."

"That's better," Rink said. "How many bodies did you guys take from here?"

"Only one. The wrong one. Some lady. We got her instead of the whore, so we came back to get the right one but she was gone. We weren't going to hurt your friend. That's all I know. I promise."

"You're sure you're not keeping anything from me?" Rink said.

"No, I promise. I wouldn't lie," the hood said.

"You guys only took one body, huh?"

"Yeah, some dead lady. The wrong one."

"There are two bodies missing," the sergeant said. "Who took the body of the whore?"

"If we were paid to take the body of the whore and we got her out of here, do you think we'd be so stupid as to come back to get her body if we already had it?" the hood said, making a mistake.

Rink didn't like his attitude.

He slid him about six inches back into the cooler.

That stimulated a predictable response.

"AAAHHHHHHHHHH! NO! NO! NO!" the cheap

crook started screaming. "I'm telling the truth! We only took one body! You can have it back!"

"This is interesting," the sergeant said. "There seems to be an epidemic of body theft going on in San Francisco."

"Are you sure this guy's telling the truth about not stealing both bodies?" Peg-leg said, adding his two cents. "Because who else would come in here on the same night and steal a body? I've been working here since 1925 and this is the first time anybody has taken a body and the chances are a million to one that two bodies would be stolen by different people on the same night. Put the son-of-a-bitch back in there and get the truth out of him."

"AAAHHHHHHHHHH!" was the hood's response to that remark.

"No, he's telling the truth," Rink said. "I know the truth when I hear it and this bastard's not lying. Look at him. Do you think there's a lie left in this quivering mass of bullshit? No, I've got him telling the truth for the first time in his life."

"Then I don't know what in the hell is happening," Peg-leg said, pretending to be angry. "Maybe there's another nut loose in San Francisco. All I know is I'm short two bodies and I want you to put it in your report that I want them back."

"OK, Peg-leg," Rink said. "Calm down. These guys have got the divorcée's body, so I've already got one of them back for you."

"You're right," Peg-leg said. "Getting one of them back is better than having both of them gone. I need dead bodies, so I can make a living."

"I know. I know," the sergeant said, walking over to the desk and getting some more coffee. He just left the hood lying there on the tray with half of his face out in the light. The hood didn't say a word about his condition. He didn't want to ruin a good thing and find himself all by his lonesome back in the dark with the dead people for company. He was going to let well enough alone.

Sergeant Rink took a sip of coffee.

"There's no reason why anybody would want to short you some bodies, is there?" Rink said to Peg-leg. "You haven't noticed anything suspicious going on around here, have you?"

"Fuck no," Peg-leg said. "This place is filled with corpses and I want that dead whore back."

"OK, OK," Sergeant Rink said. "I'll see what I can do."

He turned casually toward me.

"Do you know anything about this?" he said.

"How in the hell would I know anything about this? I just dropped by to say hello and have a cup of coffee with my old friend Peg-leg," I said.

The hood lying in the corner started to come to again. He began fluttering like a drunken butterfly.

"You didn't kick him hard enough," Rink said to the statue of a hood sitting next to him.

The statue obediently kicked him very hard in the head. The butterfly hood became unconscious again.

"Thank you," Sergeant Rink said.

The Labrador Retriever of Dead People

I started thinking about my involvement with all of this and did a quick little summary of where I was at, taking into consideration the answers Sergeant Rink had gotten from the hood on the tray.

In other words, I was thinking about my client: the beautiful rich woman who could put away the beer. She'd hired these cheap hoods to do the same thing that I was hired to do, to snatch that body. It didn't make any sense. We'd practically fallen over each other stealing a corpse, and the guy lying handcuffed on the tray had certainly gotten more than he had bargained for.

Rink returned to the slab to do a little more grilling.

"Comfortable?" he said in a motherly tone.

"Yes," the hood said, sonlike.

What else could he say?

"Here, let me make you feel a little better," Mother Rink said.

The sergeant pulled the tray out, so that you could see the hood's chest.

"Comfy?"

The hood nodded his head slowly.

"Now, what were you supposed to do with the body of that God-damn whore? What did the rich dame want done with it?"

"We were supposed to call a bar at ten o'clock and ask for a Mr. Jones and he'd tell us what we were supposed to do, then," the hood sang like a choir boy.

"Who's Mr. Jones?" Rink said.

"The guy with the fire-hydrant neck," the hood said.

"Good boy," the sergeant said. "What's the name of the bar?"

"The Oasis Club on Eddy Street."

"It's eleven now," Rink said.

He walked over to a telephone on the desk where Peg-leg was sitting. He dialed information and then he dialed the Oasis Club. "I'd like to speak to Mr. Jones." He waited for a moment and then he said, "Thank you," and hung up the telephone. He walked back over to the refrigerator.

"There's no Mr. Jones there. You're not looking for a little more time with the dead people are you?"

"No! No," the hood said. "Maybe he got tired of waiting. He said if we didn't call him then the deal was off and he'd assume that we hadn't been able to get the body. He also said something else."

"What was that?" Rink said.

"He said, 'Don't fuck up.' He really meant it."

"You should have listened to him because you guys fucked up."

"We tried. How did we know that we were taking the wrong body? They told us what slab it was on and everything. I mean, how could we go wrong?"

"Easy," Rink said. "I wouldn't hire you clowns to walk a dog."

Then Rink turned to Peg-leg.

"I wonder how the employers of these goons knew which tray the body was on," he said.

"Obviously they didn't," Peg-leg said. "Because the wrong body was snatched. Speaking of the wrong body: I want that suicide wino divorcée back and pronto."

"Where's the body?" Rink said to the hood sitting on the chair beside his freshly-unconscious friend.

"Can I speak?" the hood said. He didn't want to do anything that would get the sergeant excited. He wanted things to stay the way they were because he wasn't hand-cuffed on a tray or lying unconscious on the floor.

"You're talking right now," Rink said. "You just answered me."

"Oh, that's right," the hood said, surprised to hear his own voice speaking. "What do you want?" he said, trying it out again.

"Besides stupidity, deafness runs in your family, too, huh? I want to know where the body is, you asshole," Rink said.

"In the trunk of our car."

"Where's the car?"

"Parked around the corner," the hood said.

"Go and get the body," Rink said.

"Sure, then what?"

"What do you mean then what? Bring it back here, stupid," the sergeant said.

"You're going to let me walk out of here by myself?" the hood said, dumbfoundedly. He couldn't believe his ears.

"Why not?" Rink said. "Go and get it. You're stupid but I don't think you're crazy enough to try and take a powder on me. I'm a mean man. You want to stay on the good side of me. I'm beginning to take a liking to you, so go and get that fucking body right now."

"OK," the hood said apologetically. I don't know why he was apologetic but he was. Human behavior is hard to bet on.

A few moments later he came back lugging the laundry bag with the dead divorcée in it. He bore a great resemblance to a Labrador Retriever bringing back a duck to its master.

"You're a swell guy," Rink said. "Give that body to Peg-leg and set your ass back down."

"Thanks, boss," the hood said.

"There's one body for you, Peg-leg," Rink said. "Said case solved."

Dancing Time

Peg-leg was holding up his end of the deal perfectly. What a pal. Of course two hundred and fifty dollars cash money helps. A one-legged man can get a lot of dancing time out of that in San Francisco.

"Well, I've got to be on my way," I said. "This has been very interesting but I've got to make a living."

"That's a joke," Sergeant Rink said, then he kind of sighed. "You could have been a good detective, Card, if you hadn't spent so much time daydreaming. Oh, well . . ."

He let it drop.

I'd always been a major disappointment to him.

Rink didn't know that I was living part of my life in Babylon. To him I was just a daydreaming fuckup. I let him think that. I knew that he wouldn't be able to understand Babylon if I told him about it. He just didn't have that kind of mind, so I let it pass. I was his fuckup and that was all right. Babylon was a lot better than being a cop and having to wage the war against crime on time.

I started toward the door. I had a body out in the car that needed to be delivered, and I'd have to drive around for a while first and think about it. Things had gotten a little complicated with the entrance of the three hoods. I needed some time to think it all over. I had to make the right move.

"See you later, 'Eye,' " Peg-leg said.

"Keep your nose clean and stop being a fuckup," Rink said.

I looked over at the hood handcuffed on the slab.

He was just lying there staring up at the ceiling.

This had not been a good day for him.

The hood in the chair sat there looking as if he'd been caught with his pants down at a nuns' picnic.

The third hood lay beside him on the floor.

The electric company had turned off his lights for not paying the bill.

I think when he came to he would think twice about continuing the profession of being a hood, not unless he liked to sleep on morgue floors.

The Blindman

The car was waiting for me parked across the street from the morgue with the body of the murdered whore in the trunk. That body was my ticket to five hundred more bucks but things had gotten a little complicated.

Why had the beer-drinking rich dame hired these three hoods to steal the same body that I had been hired to steal? It didn't make sense. By doing that this whole business had been turned into a Bowery Boys' comedy with everybody falling all over everybody else, but the results hadn't been too amusing for those hoods back in the morgue.

Sergeant Rink had turned their lives into hell on earth. I shuddered when I thought about that poor son-of-a-bitch who'd been put alive into the cooler. I don't think that was his idea of fun. I think he would have preferred watching a baseball game or doing something else.

But I had spent enough time thinking about those jerks. I had more important things on my mind. What was I going to do with this God-damn body? The hoods were supposed to get in touch with the neck at a bar at ten, but he wasn't there when Sergeant Rink had called.

My appointment with the rich beer drinker and the neck was at Holy Rest Cemetery at 1 A.M. Now I had to figure out what I was going to do next. Should I keep the rendezvous?

That was my only chance to get the five hundred bucks and be able to afford an office, a secretary, a car, and be able to change the style of my life. They'd already paid me five hundred dollars for half my fee and given me three hundred dollars expense money. I still had the five hundred bucks and so I was ahead of the game anyway you looked at it.

Maybe I should just take the body and dump it in the bay and forget about meeting the people and consider myself five hundred bucks closer to having some human dignity. I could probably afford some kind of office, secretary, and car for that if I counted my pennies and made each one of them run a mile. It wouldn't be a fancy operation but at least it would be.

I didn't know what kind of weird business might happen if I kept the appointment with them. Normal people don't hire two different sets of men to steal a corpse from the morgue. That didn't make any sense at all and I had no way of anticipating what would happen if I went out to the cemetery and kept my appointment with them.

They might not even be there.

They might be in China right now for all that I knew, but if they did keep the appointment I had a gun to put a dent in any weird business they might try. That neck was a frightening human being. I'd hate to tangle with him but I did have six pieces of lead to throw at him. I wasn't a bad shot and he'd be hard to miss.

Those were my options: a sure five hundred dollars or a gamble for five hundred more with some very strange citizens, a beer-vanishing rich woman and a chauffeur with a neck the size of a herd of buffaloes.

At least I had some options.

A couple of days ago I'd been reduced to bumping into a blind beggar and knocking the cup out of his hand. I picked the money up off the sidewalk for him and he was fifty cents short when I handed his cup back to him. I think he was a very perceptive blindman because he started yelling at me, "Where's the rest of the money! It's not all here! Give me my money back, you God-damn thief!"

I had to take a quick powder.

So what I was thinking about now was a lot more interesting than the things I had been thinking about.

There are only so many blind beggars in San Francisco and the word gets around.

BABY

What in the fuck do I have to lose? I thought as I turned the key in the ignition. I'd made up my mind. I was going to deliver the body. It was now a little after eleven and I had some time to kill before I was due at Holy Rest Cemetery, so I decided to drive around for a little while. I had been without a car for a long time. I looked at the gas gauge. The tank was 3/4's full. This would be fun. I started up the engine and was off.

I headed for the Marina.

I turned the radio on.

In no time at all I was humming along to some popular song that I'd never heard before. I have a very good ear for music. I pick up tunes fast. It's one of my talents. Too bad

I never learned how to sing or play a musical instrument. I might have gone far, all the way to the top if I'd done that.

I was feeling very good.

I'd made up my mind.

I was listening to some good music.

And I had the body of a dead whore in the trunk.

What more could a man want in these troubled times? I mean, the world was at war but everything was going OK for me. I didn't have any complaints. This was my day.

As I drove up Columbus Avenue toward the Marina, I thought about being a big bandleader in Babylon with my own radio station.

"Hello, out there. This is station BABY from high atop the Hanging Gardens of Babylon. We're very happy to bring you tonight C. Card and His Big Band," the announcer would say. "And here's C. Card . . ."

"Hello, swinging cats of Babylon!" I would say. "This is your servant of sound C. Card playing music to light your dreams by, and we'll start out with Miss Nana-dirat, our songbird of forbidden pleasure, singing 'When Irish Eyes Are Smiling.' "

I was really getting the maximum amount of pleasure out of the radio. That is, until I noticed that a car was following me.

Stew Meat

The car was a 1937 black Plymouth Sedan with four black guys in it. They were very, very black and all wearing dark suits. The car looked like a piece of coal with headlights and it was definitely following me.

Who were these guys?

How had they gotten into the picture?

My few moments of radio bliss had been totally shattered. Why can't life be as simple as it could be?

There was a red light at the next intersection. I stopped and waited for it to change.

The black Plymouth filled with black men pulled up along side me and the front window next to me was rolled down. One of the black men leaned out and said in a voice deep enough to be on the *Amos 'n' Andy Show,* "We want that body. Pull over and give it to us or we'll razor you into stew meat."

"You've made a big mistake," I said through my partially rolled down window. "I don't know what you're talking about. I'm an insurance salesman for Hartford of New York."

"Don't be funny, Stew Meat," the black man said.

The light turned green and the chase was on.

It was the first car chase I'd ever been in.

I'd seen a lot of them in the movies but I'd never been in one before. It was a lot different from the ones I'd seen in the movies. First of all, I've never really been a very good driver and their driver was topnotch. Also, in the movies the car chases go on for miles. This one didn't. I made a turn a few blocks away on Lombard and crashed my car into a parked station wagon. That brought an abrupt end to the car chase. It had been interesting. Too bad it had been so short.

Fortunately, I hadn't hurt myself.

I was shaken up a little but I was OK.

The car full of black guys pulled up behind me and they jumped out. True to their promise they each had a razor, but I had a gun in my pocket, so things were not going to be as uneven as they appeared.

I slowly got out of the car. It's good to do things slowly when you've got a .38 in your pocket ready for action. I had all the time in the world.

"Where's that body, Stew Meat?" the one who had spoken before said. He was a very tough-looking hombre and so were his three dusky muchachos.

I pulled the gun out of my pocket and pointed it in their

general direction. The shoe was on a different foot now. They froze in their tracks.

"And I don't like to be called stew meat," I said, enjoying the situation. "Drop those razors."

There was the sound of four razors hitting the street. I was really ahead of the game. That is, until an old woman rushed out onto the front porch of her house and inquired into why we had ruined her car. She introduced her inquiry by screaming at the top of her lungs, "My station wagon! My station wagon! I just finished paying for it yesterday. I sent the last check in."

A dozen or so of her neighbors had poured out onto their front porches and were rapidly taking sides with the woman whose station wagon wasn't any more.

Nobody was interested in my viewpoint. I wasn't able to get a word in.

I figured the only way I could get some respite from them was to fire my gun into the air. That would drive them back into their houses and give me a minute or two to take command of the situation and do something because I sure had to do something and quick.

I aimed the gun in the air and pulled the trigger.

click

WHAT!

click click click, I kept clicking away.

IT WAS THE WRONG FUCKING GUN!

It was my gun, the empty one. The four black men went to the street for their razors. The woman was still yelling, "My station wagon! My station wagon!" The neighbors were busy joining in. The whole situation had suddenly turned into Bedlam on one of its bad days.

The black men had re-razored themselves and were coming at me. I reached into my other pocket and took out Peg-leg's gun: the one with the bullets.

"Stop!" I said to the black guys.

They looked meaner than hell except for one of them who was smiling. He was the one who'd called me "stew meat." He had a huge smile that went ear-to-ear like a pearl necklace. It sent a chill down my spine. He should meet the neck. They'd be great friends together. They had so much in common.

I could hear somebody making the introduction:

"Smile, meet Neck."

"Glad ta meetcha."

If I'd been there I would have been introduced as Stew Meat:

"Stew Meat, this is Neck."

"Hi-ya, Neck."

"My friend Smile."

"A friend of Neck's is a friend of mine."

Then I was jerked back to reality by the real voice of Smile saying, "Stew Meat, you just run outa luck."

"I'm warning you," I said.

"Hee-hee," Smile said.

He was still smiling when I shot him in the leg. That sent the woman who owned the smashed station wagon and all of her neighbors running screaming into their houses.

The smile didn't leave Smile's face but it changed from an ear-to-ear smile to a soft smile that resembled an old man getting a little Christmas present from a child. The razor dropped gently out of his hand. There was a small bloody patch on his leg that was getting bigger and bigger. The bullet had gone right through his leg about six inches above the knee. It just punched a hole in him.

The other three black men dropped their razors, too.

"Shit, Stew Meat, you just shoot me with an empty pistol," Smile said. "This ain't worth no fifty bucks. They say you just give us the body if we show you our razors. Shit, a bullet just went through my leg."

I didn't have time to console him.

I had to get out of there before the police came and brought an end to all of this. Well, my car wasn't working any more, so that left one car that was working: theirs.

"Enough of this," I said. "All of you take deep breaths right now and don't move. I'll tell you when to exhale."

They all took deep breaths and held them in.

I stepped back to Peg-leg's wrecked car and got the keys out of the ignition.

"Keep that breath in there," I warned them, waving the gun at them. I stepped around to the back of the car. I could see that the four black gentlemen were having trouble keeping their breaths in. I opened up the trunk.

"OK," I said.

They all exhaled.

"Shit," Smile said. "Shit."

"Get this body out of here," I said. I motioned toward them again with the gun and they stepped forward and removed the body. "Put it in the back seat of your car," I said. "And on the double. I don't have all day."

Smile was still smiling. It had grown a little fainter but it could still be classified as a smile. The closest description that I can think of would be to say that it was now philosophical.

192

"Shit," he said. "First, he shoot me with an empty gun, then he make me hold my breath until I get dizzy and now he steal my car."

I could still see him smiling as I drove away.

The Lone Eagle

I was about a block away when suddenly I made a left and drove the car around the block, returning to the scene of Peg-leg's wrecked car and the four bad black men. I came up behind them. They were standing there staring in the direction I had driven away.

I honked and they turned around.

I'll never forget the expression on their faces when they saw me. The three unwounded men had picked up their razors again. When they saw me the razors dropped effortlessly out of their hands and back down onto the street that was rapidly becoming their home. It seemed at this point impossible for those razors ever to make stew meat again or even come up with a shave.

They had seen their day.

The black man with the bullet hole in his leg flashed me a huge smile when he saw me. "Shit!" he said. "It's Stew Meat again. What happened this time? You come back for our pants?"

The other three black men thought that was pretty funny and they started laughing. It was pretty funny. I couldn't help from smiling myself. Except for their wanting to carve me up, these were good guys.

"No, keep your pants," I said.

"You Santa Claus," Smile said.

"Who paid you to get this body from me?" I said. "That's all I want to know."

"Why didn't you say so?" Smile said. "Shit! that's an easy one. A guy with a neck like a trunk and a flashy white doll who drank beer but didn't go piss. Where'd she put all that beer? Them da boss, but you da boss now."

"Thanks," I said.

"Shit, Stew Meat," Smile said. "Anytime, but don't shoot me no more. I'm getting too old for bullets. You don't need any partners, do ya?"

"No," I said. "I'm a lone eagle."

This time they all waved as I drove off in their car.

A Funny Building

Now what was I going to do?

When you're hired to steal a body from the city morgue, that's very strange in itself, but when the people who hire you hire other people to steal the same body from the morgue and then hire some more people to steal the body from you after you manage to steal it, you've got a lot of weirdness going on.

Why did it have to get more complicated after I'd made up my mind to go to the cemetery and see if I could get the remaining five hundred of my fee from them?

What was my next move going to be?

I still had some time before I was to keep my appointment with those people, but I'd be a fool if I did. They definitely were not to be trusted. The only thing they had going for them was the possibility of five hundred bucks.

But of course I had something they wanted very much in their weird way. I had the dead whore's body in the back seat of the just commandeered automobile of four bad black men.

Maybe I should start playing my cards a little differently.

I had been playing things too much their way.

I think I'll raise the ante, I thought to myself, *and introduce a new game.* I was going to need more money than five hundred dollars. I knew that Peg-leg was going to have a very adverse reaction to my cracking his car up. I think he was going to want a new car.

No, seeing how things were developing, five hundred was chicken feed now. If those people wanted that body, and they certainly seemed to be showing a lot of inclination in that direction, they were going to have to pay through the nose to get it.

I made a quick stop at my apartment house.

I took the body out of the back seat and slung it over my shoulder and carried it into the building. I pretended that it was a bag of laundry. My pretending didn't make any difference because nobody was there to see me. Thank God that the landlady had croaked that day. Maybe my luck wasn't so bad after all. I might come out of this with a lot more money than I had anticipated.

I smiled as I carried the dead whore's body past the stairs that led up to the apartment of the dead landlady. I thought about her body being carried down the stairs a little while earlier in the day, and now here I was carrying another dead body back into the building.

This was really a funny building.

It would make a nice little extension to add onto the morgue. Bodies were coming and going in here like letters in the post office.

I took the dead whore down the hall and into my apartment. I put her body down on the kitchen floor next to the refrigerator and then I opened the refrigerator and took all the moldy food and unidentifiable objects off the shelves.

Ugh . . .

Then I took the shelves out.

Why not?

It was the perfect place to keep her and the last place anyone would look.

The Five-hundred-dollar Foot

I was back in the car driving south out of San Francisco toward Holy Rest Cemetery and my "appointment" with the neck and his beer-drinking mistress. This was going to be an interesting meeting but it wasn't going to be the way they had planned it. We were going to play by my rules now and I had a feeling that corpse back in my refrigerator was worth a lot more than five hundred bucks.

I had the feeling that I now owned a ten-thousand-dollar dead body. I had stolen it and it was mine and I intended to get paid every dollar that it was worth and the sum of ten thousand dollars seemed just right to me.

I saw the light of a telephone booth ahead of me along the road. I remembered that I still hadn't called my mother and gotten that out of the way. I'd better take care of that before I got onto more serious business. I didn't want it preying on my mind as I was getting ready to pull off the biggest caper of my life and be put permanently on Easy Street.

I pulled over and got out.

I dropped a nickel in and dialed her number.

It rang a dozen times.

God-damn it! I didn't get to hear her answer the phone with, "Hello?" and then I'd say, "Hi, Mom. It's me," and then she'd say, "Hello? who is this speaking? Hello?" and, *"Mom,"* I'd whine, followed by, "This can't be my son calling. Hello?" continuing with me whining, *"Mom,"* and her saying, "It sounds like my son, but he wouldn't have the nerve to call if he was still a private detective."

By her not being home I was spared all that.

Where was she?

It was Friday and she'd gone to the cemetery to see my father that I'd killed when I was four, but I knew she was back from the cemetery by now.

Where was she?

I got back in the car and continued on my way to the cemetery. It was only about ten minutes away. Then the shit would hit the fan. I had the idea that the neck and his rich boss weren't going to like the new change in plans and my brand-new price for the body.

Yes, they were in for an unpleasant surprise and I couldn't think of two nicer people for it to happen to. I was very glad that I had five bullets left. That was enough to turn the neck into a little finger.

Then I remembered something.

I reached into my pocket and took out the empty revolver and put it down on the seat beside me. I wasn't going to make that mistake again. How embarrassing. That could have backfired on me if I hadn't regained control of the situation the way I did by shooting Smile in the leg.

I'd been lucky.

Shit. Smile might have been sitting where I was sitting right now at the steering wheel of his own car with his three friends in the car, joking and laughing, the whore's body in the trunk, and I could be lying in the street as part of an unfinished recipe. All you would need to finish it would be some onions, potatoes, carrots and a bay leaf.

I didn't like the idea of being stew.

The Night
Is Always Darker

It was really a dark night as I drove toward
Holy Rest Cemetery. It was so dark that I thought about my
serial *Smith Smith Versus the Shadow Robots*. When Professor Abdul Forsythe got the mercury crystals and was able
to activate his piles of poor unfortunate shadow victims and
set them marching upon the world, the results would look
like this.

The Professor-Abdul-Forsythe artificial night would resemble the kind of night that I was driving through to get
to the cemetery.

Then another thought crossed my mind jerking me back
from Babylon. Perhaps the night is always darker when

you're on your way to a cemetery in it. That was something to think about, but not for long because my mind was immediately returned to Babylon.

BZZZZZZZZZZZZZZZZZZZ

It was my beautiful eternal secretary Nana-dirat on the intercom.

"Hello, doll," I said. "What's up?"

"It's for you, lover," she said in her breathless voice.

"Who is it?" I said.

"It's Dr. Francis, the famous humanitarian."

"What does he want?"

"He won't tell me. He says that he can only speak to you."

"OK, doll," I said. "Put him on."

"Hello, Mr. Smith Smith," Dr. Francis said. "I'm Dr. Francis."

"I know who you are," I said. "What do you want? Time is money."

"Excuse me?" the doctor said.

"I'm a busy man," I said. "Give it to me straight. I can't waste my time."

"I want to hire you."

"That's what I was waiting to hear," I said. "My fee is one pound of gold a day plus expenses."

"That sounds reasonable for a man of your reputation as a private investigator," Dr. Francis said.

"You've heard of me?" I said, playing it coy.

"All of Babylon has heard of you," he said.

I of course knew that. I just wanted to hear him say it. I had a delightful ego problem.

"Now what can I do for you?" I said. There was a pause at the other end of the line. "Dr. Francis?" I said.

"Is it all right for me to speak freely over the telephone?" he said. "I mean, nobody could be listening in?"

"Don't worry," I said. "If anybody does any telephone tapping in Babylon it's usually me. Tell me what your problem is."

Little did I know that the diabolical Professor Abdul Forsythe was listening to our conversation. I had been a little too glib with my telephone-tapping joke and it was to cause me a lot of trouble later on.

"Well, Mr. Smith Smith," Dr. Francis said.

"Just call me Smith," I said. "Everybody does."

"Smith, I have reason to believe that somebody is trying to steal my latest invention and use it for evil purposes."

"What's your invention?" I said.

"I've invented mercury crystals," Dr. Francis said.

"I'll be right over," I said.

I had been afraid this was going to happen: that somebody would come along and invent mercury crystals. I frankly didn't think the world was ready for it yet. After all, this was the year 596 B.C. and the world had a lot of growing up to do.

Smiley's Genuine Louisiana Barbecue

SSSCCCRRREEEEEECCCHHH!!!

I slammed on the brakes.

Babylon almost caused me to drive right past the cemetery. I pulled over and stopped and turned my lights out. I didn't see any other cars there. If anyone was coming I'd arrived first. I didn't even know if the neck and its beer-drinking keeper were going to show up, but I had a hunch they would. That's why I was there. Now I'd just wait and see what happened. You don't get a chance at ten thousand dollars every day.

Suddenly I was curious about something.

I reached into my pocket and took out a match.

I lit it and read the registration on the steering wheel: Smiley's Genuine Louisiana Barbecue.

That figured.

I'd have to stop in and visit Smiley someday and try some of his barbecue. It would really be worth it to see the expression on his face when he saw me coming through the door.

I blew out the match and waited in the dark for a while.

I started to think about Babylon but I was able to wrestle it out of my mind by carefully not being impressed by how dark it was. That could lead me very easily back to Babylon. If I thought about the darkness, I'd soon be thinking about the shadow robots, and that wouldn't do at all.

I didn't want Babylon to put me behind the eight ball again. I was lucky that I saw the cemetery. I could have driven halfway to Los Angeles and be on Chapter Seven of *Smith Smith Versus the Shadow Robots.* Then I never would have had a chance at finding my client and getting ten thousand dollars. All I would have ended up with was a dead whore in my refrigerator.

That's what you would hardly call the successful conclusion of a case.

Into the Cemetery We Will Go

I had been sitting there—I don't know how long—when a car came down the road. It was the only traffic that I had seen. The car was driving very slowly. It looked as if its destination was the cemetery.

It was too far away to tell what kind of car it was. Anyway, I couldn't tell. I wondered if it was the Cadillac limousine. The car stopped two hundred yards down the road from me. The headlights went black and some people got out of the car. They had a flashlight but I couldn't make out who they were. It could be the neck and blonde company or just some plain ordinary grave robbers.

I had no way of knowing until I got out of the car and became a stealthful confident private eye starting to conclude the biggest deal of his life, so that's what I did. I got out of the car.

I was lacking only one thing: a flashlight.

Then I got an idea.

I got back into the car and opened up the glove compartment.

Bonanza!

A flashlight!

This was a sign from heaven.

Everything was going to work out OK.

I was supposed to meet the neck and Our Lady of the Limitless Bladder by a monument to some fallen soldiers of the Spanish-American War. The monument was about three hundred yards into the cemetery. It was only a little ways away from my father's grave.

I had passed that monument many times visiting his grave. I sure wish I hadn't killed him. Perhaps if everything worked out with this case, I might have a few moments left over at the end of it to do a little mourning for him. Why did I throw that ball out into the street? I wish I had never seen that ball!

With the flashlight in one hand, I didn't have it on, but it was ready to stab a ray of light if I should need it, and the loaded gun in my other hand, I slipped into the cemetery and made my way among the graves toward the Spanish-American War monument.

I moved with a great deal of caution.

Surprise was a very important element in this situation and I wanted it on my side. I had to cut through a grove of trees to get to the monument. It was just on the other side of the trees. I had to be careful going through the trees. It was very dark and I didn't want to fall down and make a lot of noise. When I got into the trees, I measured every step as if it were my last.

I was halfway through the trees, moving like a shadow, when I heard voices coming from the direction of the monument about fifty yards in front of me.

I couldn't quite make out what they were saying but there were three of them: two men and a woman. I was too far away to recognize them. The trees muffled their sound.

I took ten more very careful steps forward and then stopped for a few seconds and collected my thoughts and tried to make out what they were saying and who it was but they were still too far away.

I had a haunted feeling that this case was rapidly coming to a close. Something was not right. I started moving forward again. Every step was an eternity. I wished I was in Babylon, holding hands with Nana-dirat.

The Surprise

This is what I saw when finally I was positioned in the trees to see what was happening at the monument: The first thing I saw was Sergeant Rink standing there, holding a flashlight in his hand.

I stood in the trees out of sight staring at him.

He was the last person in the world I expected to see there. I was dumbfounded. What in the hell was happening?

The next thing I saw was the neck and its beer-guzzling mistress standing there, fastened together by a pair of handcuffs. The neck looked very unhappy. The rich blonde looked as if she needed a beer really bad, which in her case meant a case.

Rink was in full control of the situation.

He was talking to them.

"All I want to know is why did you murder the girl and then try to steal her body from the morgue? When you killed her you could have taken the body away with you. It doesn't make any sense. I can't figure it out. Stealing that body is what caused you to be caught."

"We have nothing to say," the neck said.

"Who said I wanted to hear from you?" Rink said. "I'm talking to the lady here. She's the one who ran this show, so you keep your mouth zipped or I'll take care of it for you."

The neck started to say something and then changed his mind. Sergeant Rink's presence could cause that.

"Well, lady, tell me the truth and I can make it easier on you. Nobody really cares about a murdered whore. At the most it can only cost you a few years if you level with me."

Rink waited.

Finally she spoke, wetting her lips first.

"Listen, fat cop," she said. "First, these handcuffs are too tight. Second, I want a beer. Third, I'm rich and it's already easy for me. And fourth, you can't prove a thing. All you've got is a chain of circumstantial evidence that my lawyers will blow away like a summer breeze. After they get you on the stand and are through with you, the police department will retire you as a mental defective. Either that or your next case will be cleaning up after the horses at the police stables. Are things a little clearer now?"

Nobody had ever called Sergeant Rink a fat cop before.

He stood there unable to believe it.

He had made his bet and he had been called.

"Think it over," she said. Then she looked down at her

handcuffed wrist with a very sophisticated expression of exasperation. After that she looked into the sergeant's eyes. She did not look away.

I just stood there like somebody in a movie theater watching it all happen in front of my eyes. The price of admission was only a trip to the cemetery at midnight in a stolen car after having shot a Negro in the leg and then stopping at my apartment and putting the body of a murdered prostitute in my refrigerator.

That's all.

"I think you're bluffing," Sergeant Rink said.

"You can't be as stupid as you look," the rich blonde said. "Do you know what twenty-five years of horse shit looks like?"

The sergeant had to think that one over. Rink was a very smart detective but he had met his match. He didn't have any more cards up his sleeve.

Too bad I had been out of earshot when Sergeant Rink was telling them his evidence. That would have given me some idea of what was going on. Right now I hadn't the slightest idea. I was totally in the dark.

I was still stunned to see Sergeant Rink there. How in the hell had he found out where we were to meet? It baffled the imagination. I had expected the possibility of seeing the neck and its rich pal, but the sergeant never.

Then Rink shook his head slowly and reached into his pocket for the key to the handcuffs. He walked over and released the neck and the blonde. The sergeant didn't look too happy.

The rich woman rubbed her wrist and then looked at the sergeant sort of sympathetically. "It was a nice try," she said.

The neck started to growl.

It liked having the upper hand now.

"Shut up, Mr. Cleveland," she said.

The neck stopped growling and changed from a bear into a lamb.

"Well," Sergeant Rink said. "You can't win them all. At least if I'm going to lose, I like losing to some class."

The socialite smiled at the servant of the law.

The neck trying to please its owner smiled, too. But it failed miserably. Its smile resembled a movie marquee advertising a horror film.

"How about a beer, Sergeant?" she said, smiling. "There's a tavern back down the road." She held out her hand toward him. Rink looked at it for a few seconds and then gave it a good friendly shake.

"Sure," he said. "Let's go have a beer."

Boy, did he have a surprise coming.

Good-bye, $10,000

After they had gone to get a beer, I just stood there for a few moments. There went my prospects for wealth. Good-bye, $10,000. That body in my refrigerator wasn't worth a penny now.

I walked out of the trees over to the monument dedicated to those who had fallen in the Spanish-American War. I felt as if I were one of them.

Oh, well, I still had five hundred bucks in my pocket.

I wouldn't be able to have all the things that I had envisioned like a fine office and a beautiful secretary and a good car, so I'd have to compromise. I'd have a small office, a plain secretary and a Model A.

I was standing by the monument, lost in thought, thinking about all of this when I was rudely surprised by the sudden appearance of four black men all carrying razors.

"Hi, Stew Meat," Smiley said, who was limping at the head of them. He had a tie wrapped around his leg just above the bullet hole.

Where in the hell did they come from?

"We thought we'd pick up our car and get a nice thank you for da loan of it," he said. Smiley had a huge smile on his face. He had something up the sleeve of that smile. "Also, Stew Meat. We need dat money in your pocket for expenses and don't reach for dat gun you shot me with or we cut you real bad, Stew Meat."

Ah, shit. I didn't care any more. Everything had gotten to be a little bit too much for me. I reached toward my pocket.

"Careful now," Smiley said, still smiling. "I sorta like you even if you did shoot me in the leg. Don't disappoint me now."

I very slowly reached in my pocket and took out the money. It was a nice roll: a few dreams. I flipped it to him.

"Good, Stew Meat," Smiley said.

He looked at the money.

"Five C's," he said.

"What about the girl's body?" I said. "Still want it?"

"Naa, you can have it, Stew Meat."

"What now?" I said, expecting some wear and tear on my body from the four black men. After all, I had shot their head man in the leg and I had stolen their car. Some people take offence at things like that.

"This is enough, Stew Meat. I like you," Smiley said. "We got da money. We got paid. The bullet didn't break the bone. Just went clean through. We leave you alone. Bygones be da bygones."

"You're OK, Smiley," I said. "How's your barbecue?"

"Da best," Smiley smiled. "Stop by. I'll give you some ribs. On the house."

And off they went.

It's Midnight.
It's Dark.

I was standing beside the monument to the fallen of the Spanish-American War, alone again, having watched my little office, plain secretary and Model A vanish into thin air.

Thank God I still had a wonderful office with a sunken marble bath, the most beautiful woman in the world, and a golden chariot in Babylon.

That was the consolation prize.

"Son!" I heard a voice yell coming toward me from behind some tombstones. "Son!" I recognized the voice. It was my mother. She came hurrying up to me, almost out of breath.

"What are you doing here?" I said in a numb voice.

217

"You know this is the day I always visit the father and husband you murdered. You know that. Why do you ask that?"

"It's midnight," I said. "It's dark."

"I know that," she said. "But do the dead know that? No, they don't. I just stayed a little longer than usual. But why are you here? You never visit your father any more."

"It's a long story."

"Are you still being that private detective, chasing people with bad shadows? When are you going to pay the money you owe me? You bastard!"

Sometimes Mother liked to call me a bastard.

I was used to it.

"Now that you're here, go say something to the man you murdered. Ask him forgiveness," she said, marching me over to his grave.

I stood there in front of his grave, wishing at the age of four I hadn't thrown a red rubber ball out into the street while playing with him on a Sunday afternoon in 1918 and he hadn't run after it, right into the front of a car and stuck to the grill. The undertaker had to peel him off.

"I'm sorry, Daddy," I said.

"You should be," my mother said. "What a naughty boy. Your daddy's probably a skeleton now."

Good Luck

My mother and I walked back across the cemetery to the other side where her car was parked.

We didn't say anything as we walked along.

That was good.

It gave me some time to think about Babylon. I picked up where I left off in my serial *Smith Smith Versus the Shadow Robots*. After I'd finished talking to the good Dr. Francis, I gave my secretary a passionate kiss on the mouth.

"What's that for?" she said, a little breathless afterward.

"Good luck," I said.

"Whatever happened to the good old rabbit's foot?" she said.

I took a long lustful look at her moist delicious mouth.

"Are you kidding?" I said.

"I guess not," she said. "If that's replaced rabbits' feet for luck, I want some more."

"Sorry, babe," I said. "But I've got work to do. Somebody has invented mercury crystals."

"Oh, no," she said, the expression on her face changing to apprehension.

I put my sword shoulder holster on underneath my toga.

"Watch out, son!" my mother said as I almost walked straight into an open, freshly-dug grave. Her voice jerked me back from Babylon like pulling a tooth out of my mouth without any Novocaine.

I avoided the grave.

"Be careful," she said. "Or I'll have to visit both of you out here. That would make Friday a very crowded day for me."

"OK, Mom, I'll watch my step."

I had to, seeing that I was right back where I started, the only difference being that when I woke up this morning, I didn't have a dead body in my refrigerator.

THE END